I0619420

Echoes of the Empire

Soraya Radfield

Published by Soraya Radfield, 2025.

This is a work of fiction. Similarities to real people, places, or events are entirely coincidental.

ECHOES OF THE EMPIRE

First edition. November 30, 2025.

ISBN: 978-1764102827

Written by Soraya Radfield.

Also by Soraya Radfield

The Last Conversation
Echoes of the Empire

Table of Contents

Prologue - The Moment She Burnt

A forgotten Gulf port, Circa late 12th century CE

The flames came quickly. Faster than they should have.

Vellichi pressed the scroll flat with her palm, whispering to it as if words could hold the fibres together. The ink had begun to run, salt and soot smudging the characters she had copied by lamplight only hours earlier. She knew the shape of every symbol, the weight of every curve. Not just script, but memory.

Above her, the roof groaned. Cracks split across the painted beams as if the gods themselves were fracturing.

In the courtyard beyond, the sound of feet and shouting. Not soldiers, at least not uniformed. That was how they had come. Not in banners, but in shadows. Through the back doors. Through trust.

A deep tremor ran through the compound, and dust rained down. Somewhere, a bell tolled. The sound of it hitting stone felt final.

She closed her eyes for a moment, bracing herself on the low stone table. Beneath the fear, deeper than the fear, was grief. Old, hollowed-out grief. The kind that arrives not in sharp cries, but in silence. The kind that has waited lifetimes for release.

She had been born to write. But she would die to remember.

Vellichi, daughter of tides, keeper of sacred breath, last voice of an order that had no name in common tongues. She had walked through the world with this scroll hidden beneath her ribs. Lanka. Puhar. Alexandria. Not for coin. Not for a favour. For the women whose names had been scrubbed from stone and swallowed by smoke.

Tonight, her name would join them.

The scroll was small, tightly bound with red thread. The seal, a coiled serpent, had cracked from the heat, but the symbol remained. Watching. Waiting. It had always been said the serpent did not forget.

She felt the fire approach before she heard it. A rush of air, then the low hiss of something sacred being undone.

He stepped into the doorway then, silent beneath the smoke.

She didn't turn. She didn't need to. She had known the moment the fire began that it was him.

"You came," she said, her voice steady.

He stood there, rain on his cloak, ash in his eyes.

"I didn't want to."

"Then why are you here?"

He hesitated. "If they find it, they'll use it. Twist it. Burn more than just walls."

"I know." She lifted the scroll slowly, holding it to her chest. "That's why it must disappear."

He stepped forward. "I told them you would not give it up."

"You were right."

There was no fight between them. That was the worst part. No raised voices, no rage. Only that terrible silence, the kind shared by those who had once loved across lives.

She turned and walked to the altar. Her fingers found the small stone plate, hidden beneath the offerings. A niche carved generations ago. She had always known it was there. Just as she had always known, this moment would come.

She placed the scroll inside, pressed the cover closed, and whispered something only the stone could hold.

"I forget now."

Not a plea. A vow.

"I forget... until the time returns."

The doorway behind her cracked. She didn't look back.

The fire roared through the archway, catching the old cloth hangings, and then the cedar beams above. A rush of heat swept through the sanctum, and the serpent seal glowed for one brief, defiant moment before vanishing into flame.

As the roof gave way and the night filled with fire, the wind rose, not just from sea or storm, but from somewhere older. It lifted the ash, curled around her name, and carried it out beyond the burning.

It did not carry her to death.

It carried her into breath.

She heard the vow echo as the flames claimed her:
Forget. Until the time returns.

Chapter One - The Empire Knows Her Name

Parkville Campus, University of Melbourne, Australia — Morning – Present Day

The University of Melbourne's Parkville campus was a city within a city, grand, contradictory, quietly breathing the past through sandstone arches and creaking corridors. Some buildings wore glass and steel, like declarations of progress. But others, like the wing that housed the School of Historical and Philosophical Studies, still stood in weathered bluestone, ivy threaded through old mortar-like veins in ancient skin.

Selena Ravenscroft held a hybrid role, part-time lecturer in maritime history within the School, and research fellow attached to the Grimwade Centre for Cultural Materials Conservation, where she studied early Tamil maritime artefacts, scriptural seals, and their preservation. It was a niche corner of academia, tucked between the disciplines that drew funding and the ones that drew silence. She liked it there. She belonged in the margins.

This morning, the archive room hummed with a hush that only serious scholars respected. Not quite a library, not quite a lab, more a sanctuary for the forgotten. Narrow shelves towered over hardwood tables, paper tags fluttering like faded flags from decades-old folders. An antique lamp hummed above her desk, casting a warm glow over palm-leaf fragments and microfilm scans.

Outside, the fig trees trembled in the breeze. Inside, the past was beginning to stir.

This was where Selena felt most herself; at least, until recently.

Now, even these walls had begun whispering back.

It was early still, but Selena had already been seated for hours, hunched over a flickering screen that cast her face in cold blue light. The silence in the room was weighted, broken only by the occasional shuffle of notes or the mechanical blink of microfilm reels rewinding.

Dr Suresh Subramaniam leaned over her shoulder, the scent of his clove soap catching in the still air. Former professor, now colleague and mentor, he had guided her through her first archaeological field study. Their bond was one of deep respect, layered with unspoken affection and intellectual rivalry.

"There, Lena", he said, tapping the magnified script on the screen with a practised hand. "That fragment. Look closely."

She adjusted the contrast. The ink was faint, but the ancient Grantha script held its shape:

"Kadal Magal."

Daughter of the Sea.

Selena's breath paused in her throat.

Suresh stepped back, arms folded. "It appears again here, see, and centuries later, in a Venetian spice register. Always concerning coastal trade, always unnamed. Not a person. A title."

Selena sat back, slowly. "So, she wasn't one woman?!"

5

He nodded. "Or she was the first. The name carried like a tide invoked, not inherited. Think matrilineal memory rather than dynastic succession."

Selena traced the line with one fingertip. Her skin tingled, as though the ink held heat.

Dr Suresh continued, "We've found traces in Alexandria, Suakin, southern Oman. It's always the same, temple-trained women sent between empires. Ambassadors in veils. The Cholas knew how to move quietly, especially through women no one expected."

A smile flickered across her lips. "So the sea carried secrets too."

Suresh returned her smile, but it faded quickly. "You've looked pale lately, Lena. Don't tell me you've started dreaming about the scroll again."

She didn't answer.

Instead, she stared at the word. *Kadal Magal.* And beneath it, barely legible, another script was scratched faintly in Aramaic.

"I've been seeing things," she admitted, voice low. "Not hallucinations....just... moments that feel more like remembering than thinking. Is that mad?"

Suresh didn't reply immediately. His gaze softened. "It's not madness. But it's dangerous to let memory masquerade as proof."

Fitzroy Apartment — Afternoon Rain

Back in her Fitzroy flat, a three-bedroom unit, tucked above a bookshop and two cafés that never seemed to sleep, the afternoon rain had softened into a fine mist, threading itself through the flyscreen and into her bones. Outside, the tramlines hummed along Brunswick Street, weaving through a blur of art galleries, record stores, and hidden courtyards blooming with jacaranda. Fitzroy always felt like it belonged to another time, bohemian yet scholarly, raw but poetic. It suited her; a place where contradictions could live side by side.

She wrapped herself in an old sky blue cardigan, one shoulder falling bare, and stared through the open window as a cyclist disappeared into the fog. The scent of rain on concrete mingled with cardamom from the café below. Somewhere across the rooftops, a saxophone played, a few soft notes, then silence. Melbourne held its moods like memories. And today, it felt like something was trying to be remembered.

The flat was more spacious than most in Fitzroy: a split across high ceilings and honeyed floorboards that creaked like old ships. One room was her sanctuary, soft throws, incense trays, worn paperbacks stacked beside the bed like sleeping companions. Another had become her home office, crammed with maps, transcripts, and annotated prints. The third was always made up for guests, often friends from Brisbane or Sydney who needed a few nights in the city, or those from Milan and Lisbon, who still drifted in and out of her life since her postgraduate days in Italy and the long, wandering gap year across Europe.

She tried to distract herself, to pin the phrase *Daughter of the Sea* back inside its academic box, to stop it from breathing. But it wouldn't. It followed her like salt air in the lungs, familiar and impossible to explain.

But it had already slipped through.

Flash Memory — The Seal Awakens

She opened the drawer beside her bed and stared at the terracotta seal replica. It sat in a linen pouch, edges worn from her handling, though she rarely admitted how often she reached for it. Clay cast, museum-stamped, technically harmless, no more dangerous than a paperweight. And yet, every time her fingers closed around its surface, a knot formed low in her belly, like something ancient stirring awake.

She took it out now and turned it over in her palm. The seal was no larger than a child's hand, oval and slightly concave, the clay a muted rust-red with flecks of sand clinging to its grain. Along the rim, the markings remained sharp, Tamil script braided with an unfamiliar swirl of Aramaic, like two languages learning to breathe together. In the centre, the serpent coiled, neither threatening nor benign. Just watching. Waiting. Eternal.

Her thumb grazed the edge of the serpent's curve, and then everything shifted.

Salt. Heat. The creak of a ship's wood beneath her feet. For a heartbeat, she was standing on the deck of something ancient, the horizon split between fire and water. A man's voice, low, worn, almost kind, rose in her mind like surf breaking against stone.

"Do not forget the name."

Then silence.

She gasped, the seal slipping from her hand and landing with a dull *thud* on the bedsheet. The room was still, impossibly still, except for her breath, which came in sharp, startled bursts.

It was just an object, she told herself. Just fired Earth and memory.

But somehow, it remembered her better than she remembered herself.

Fitzroy Apartment — Evening

Her phone buzzed.

Soren, her yoga instructor, her guide through the fragile seams of the self, had left a voicemail.

"Lena, checking in. I know the seal's resurfaced something. Don't try to contain it too tightly. Call me, even if it's just to sit in silence."

She didn't return the call. Instead, she pulled her cardigan closer and lit a single sandalwood candle. The scent wrapped her slowly. Familiar. Soothing. Dangerous.

That night, the dream was waiting for her.

....

Dream Trace — Chola Port, Circa 11th Century CE

Salt.

Stone.

Smoke, curling in blue lines over the sea.

She stood at the edge of a Chola port, not reconstructed, not imagined, but pulsing with life. The scent struck her first: brine and jasmine, wet wood, cumin, and sandal smoke curling from temple braziers. Then sound, the rhythmic clatter of loading crates, the creak of moored ships, a conch horn echoing from a stone archway carved with lions. This was no memory held at arm's length. It was happening.

The docks heaved with bodies. Merchants in indigo-dyed tunics bartered beside carved stone counters, their fingers stained with ink and betel nut. Sailors, half-naked and slick with sweat, hauled ropes, chanted in cadence, their oiled hair twisted into thick knots. Women in bright silk wraps, emerald, saffron, lapis, moved between market stalls, balancing baskets of turmeric root, dried myrrh, and pale river pearls. Children darted between spice carts. A white bull wandered freely, garlanded with marigold and streaked with ash.

Monsoon clouds gathered low on the horizon, their bellies swollen and dark, brooding like old gods. A metallic scent hung in the air, the promise of rain, or battle, or both.

She wore a long indigo veil that wrapped around her head and fell down her arms in gentle folds, edged with copper-thread embroidery that shimmered when the light touched it just right. Her sandals slapped lightly against the wet stone as she walked, measured and silent. Every movement was deliberate. The bangles along her wrists clicked softly, bronze, carnelian, carved bone, not for beauty, but for purpose: to speak in sound when silence was law.

Beneath the folds of her cloak, her fingers gripped a palm-leaf scroll bound in oil cloth and sealed at both ends with coiled twin serpents, a symbol not shown in open daylight. The scroll was still warm from the ritual fire it had passed through before being entrusted to her. She could feel the weight of it not in her arms, but in her ribs, as if it knew her breath, and matched it.

And then he was there.

No announcement. No footfall.

Just a shift in the air, the hairs rising along her forearm.

He stepped through the veil of incense as if the world had parted for him. Cloaked in deep grey, the hem of his robe sodden from rain that hadn't yet fallen. His face, half-hidden beneath a travel-stained hood. But his presence, unmistakable. A gravity she had felt in dreams, in ritual, in rooms long gone.

Their eyes met, for the time to fold.

He bowed. "Daughter of the Waves," he said.

The title echoed across lifetimes.

She knew him. Though his name did not surface, the ache of their separation already lived between them. He was her reflection in water, not always visible, but always felt.

"You were not expected," he said softly.

"Neither were you," she replied.

No anger. Just recognition. And loss.

She reached for the scroll at her waist, but the moment dissolved, the market noise melting into silence, the sky turning white.

....

Fitzroy Apartment — Night

Selena sat upright in bed, heart thudding hard and fast against her ribs. Her breath came in short, dry bursts, as though she'd been running, not in sleep, but across some forgotten shoreline. The room was dark, silent, but the scent of cardamom still hung in the air, delicate and persistent, like a visitor that hadn't quite left.

She brought a trembling hand to her lips. The taste of salt lingered.

Not imagined. Not poetic. Salt. Real and metallic on her tongue, as if she'd swallowed seawater in her sleep.

She blinked up at the ceiling, the shadows shifting like waves across the plaster. That had not been a dream. Not entirely.

Her body felt electric. Not scared, not quite. But wired, shaken, as though something essential had been stirred loose from her chest and hadn't found its way back in.

She reached for her phone on the nightstand, hesitated, then unlocked it.

"Hey Ani, I know it's late, but something just happened. Can we talk soon? It felt... real. Not like a memory. More like a place I just returned from."

She hit send. The little dots blinked once, then disappeared.

Ani Patel, her therapist and sometime anchor, had been with her since the burnout years — calm-voiced, fiercely perceptive, the kind of person who could name a feeling before Selena found the words for it. She trusted Ani more than she trusted her own mind at times like these. Ani had seen her cracked open before and had never once tried to seal her back too quickly.

She opened another thread. Leila, the kind of friend who didn't need small talk or preamble, just truth.

"I know you're probably asleep, but I just had the strangest experience. I think I dreamt in another language. I think I was someone else. And it felt like... home."

Selena lowered the phone into her lap, spine curling forward, the sheet slipping off her shoulder. The air had changed. She could feel it, not outside, but in her. Something had shifted. Opened.

She wasn't sure what scared her more, the fact that it had happened, or the part of her that was already hoping it would happen again.

University of Melbourne — Morning After

In the morning, an email from Dr Suresh blinked on her screen.

Subject line: *Found this in the temple archive run-off —
thought of you.*

He was just two floors below, in the South Asian
antiquities wing at Melbourne Uni. But he still sent her
discoveries the way he did everything else, methodically, with
understatement, as if he didn't want to seem too interested in
the strangeness of her research.

She opened the attachment.

The carving was delicate, no larger than a folded palm leaf.
An ivory panel, yellowed at the edges, was almost translucent.
A veiled woman stood facing an ocean swell, the hem of her
robe encircled by twin serpent tails that coiled like ink in water.
Her face was turned slightly away, carved in profile. There was
no inscription. No name. Just presence. As though she was not
meant to be described, but only remembered.

Selena sat back in her chair. Her hands felt clammy. The
image sat open on the screen, quietly breathing.

She clicked it off.

She had gone looking for history. Names, routes, timelines.

Now it was looking back.

Fitzroy — Evening

Later that evening, Fitzroy pulsed with a different rhythm,
rain tapping on tramlines, conversations rising and falling
between brick walls, fairy lights tangled in laneway trees.
Selena met Leila at Neptune's Parlour, a cosy bar carved into
what used to be a wine merchant's warehouse, tucked behind
Johnston Street. Candles flickered on the weathered bar tops,
and the windows blurred with mist.

Leila was already there, perched on a velvet stool, a half-drunk negroni in her hand. She looked up as Selena entered, her warm eyes sharpening.

"You look like someone who's seen a ghost."

Selena managed a smile as she slid into the seat opposite. "Not quite. But maybe someone I used to be."

Leila raised a brow, but didn't press. Not yet. That was the gift of their friendship, no rush, just space. They sipped in silence for a few moments. The bar hummed around them; low music, laughter, the faint clink of ice on glass.

Selena broke first. "I had a dream last night. But it didn't feel like a dream. More like... a place I'd returned to."

Leila tilted her head, intrigued but cautious. "Like déjà vu?"

"No. It was visceral. My feet were wet from the docks. My hands hurt from carrying a scroll I didn't write, but knew by heart. And today..."

She reached into her coat pocket and slid her phone across the table. The ivory carving glowed faintly on the screen.

Leila leaned in, studied the image. "Is that... you?"

Selena didn't answer. She didn't need to.

Outside, the rain pressed its fingertips to the windows, as if listening in.

Inside, Leila's voice dropped to a whisper. "What happens next?"

Selena exhaled slowly, her fingers resting near the base of her glass.

"I think... the past just found my address."

And from somewhere just beyond language, she heard it.

"Vellichi."

Her name. Not the one she was born with, the one the sea had carried back.

She didn't understand it yet,
but the empire remembered her.
Do not forget her name.

Selena's Diary Entry:

Field Notes – University of Melbourne / Fitzroy Apartment

Mission:

Research breakthrough: "Kadal Magal" / "Daughter of the Sea" appears across Tamil–Red Sea–Venetian documents. Not a singular identity — possibly a matrilineal lineage or spiritual title across centuries.

Seal still active. Triggers sensations: creaking wood, ritual fire, male voice: "Do not forget the name."

Ivory carving (Dr Suresh) shows robed woman facing a wave.

Twin serpent motif. No inscription. Presence only.

Emotional state:

Restless. Dislocated. Like being watched by time itself.

Ani and Leila are starting to worry. I haven't told them everything.

Keywords:

- Chola–Alexandria trade link
- Sea as archive
- Serpent = guardian, not threat
- Ivory carving — veiled woman facing the wave
- Seal still active; tactile trigger persists
- This is not study anymore. This is memory turned inside out.

Chapter Two: The Mind Unquiet

Fitzroy, Melbourne. The hour before sunrise – Two days earlier

Before the ivory carving. Before the email from Suresh.

The air was dry and humming with early spring heat. Light filtered through the slats of the blinds in thin, fractured lines, striping the floor of Selena Ravencroft's flat like a memory caught in shadow.

She sat cross-legged on the wooden floor, coffee gone cold beside her, fingers hovering over the linen wrap that held the terracotta seal. She had promised herself she wouldn't touch it again today. But something about it kept whispering at the edge of her thoughts, not in words, but in sensation. A tug, low and persistent, like the tide pulling from deep under the sand.

Her flat was still, too still indeed. No sound but the tick of the clock and the throb of distant traffic. It was Sunday, yet she couldn't relax. Couldn't stop, not since the archive trip down the coast.

What should have been a routine catalogue, some minor finds, review a shipment from a now-defunct maritime museum, nod politely at coastal councillors, instead, buried in a box of mislabelled clay weights and corroded coins, she'd found it.

A terracotta seal, no larger than her palm. Ancient, yet familiar in the way that dreams are half-remembered but weighted with meaning.

The first time she'd touched it, something in her body had gone still. Not lightning bolt, no strange voices, just a sharp awareness. A pause so complete it had unsettled her more than fear.

She hadn't told anyone. Not her colleagues. Not even her therapist, Ani. And certainly not her mother, who already thought her daughter's job sounded like it belonged in a monastery in an underground vault.

Just two days before the coastal visit, she had received confirmation of the new research grant; six months' funding to investigate maritime connections between the Chola empire and the Mediterranean world. A project she'd proposed half-ironically, assuming it would be rejected for being "too speculative." The committee had surprised her.

But maybe she shouldn't have been surprised. The ocean had always carried more than just goods; it ferried myths, language, and people. And somewhere along those ancient routes, between Tamilakam, modern-day South India and Alexandria, a seal like this had been pressed into wet clay and passed from one hand to another.

The Cholas weren't just warriors or temple patrons. They were seafarers. Diplomats. Traders with links stretching across the Indian Ocean, into Arabia, East Africa, and even Rome. That much, the records showed fragmented, yes, but persistent. What the records didn't show was who she had been, in the spaces between those accounts.

Her father would have asked questions, though the sort that turned over a mystery just to see how it sounded in the light. She missed that about him. Charles Ravencroft had been every bit the Oxbridge-trained historian he appeared to be, bowtie, typewriter, and all, but he had a gentle awe for mystery. He would have called the seal "a curious convergence of forgotten intention."

Her mother would've called it "old clay with too much energy."

Both would've been right.

Selena exhaled and stood, sliding the seal back into its wrap and placing it carefully beneath a stack of journals. The air in the flat had grown close, heavy. She needed out, not far, but just... away from herself.

Carlton Gardens, Melbourne — Morning

Carlton Gardens unfolded before her like a breathing canvas, the kind touched by a painter's gentlest brush. Sunlight spilled through the towering elms and Moreton Bay figs in broken, golden shafts, dappling the gravel path with shifting patterns that moved as the breeze stirred above. The scent of crushed eucalyptus leaves mingled with warm earth and the faint trace of jasmine from somewhere unseen. A magpie warbled in the distance. Water trickled from the fountain basin, catching the light like fractured glass.

Selena moved slowly beneath the trees, her footsteps muffled by soft gravel. She wore a slate-grey wool coat left unbuttoned, and beneath it, a high-neck jumper the colour of old parchment, the fabric lightweight and worn at the sleeves. A long silk scarf, rust-red with copper threads, was wrapped once around her neck and trailed slightly behind her, lifting now and then in the breeze. Her dark hair, loose at the ends, brushed the collar as she walked, and her boots, simple ankle-length leather, carried the scent of the coast from the week before.

She reached the stone bench beneath the fig tree, ran her hand along its edge, and then sat. Her fingers, ungloved, pressed briefly into her lap, grounding. The air was crisp but not cold, and everything around her felt vividly alive; the garden, the light, the earth underfoot, as if the place were listening, too.

Her thoughts moved in loops. Always have. It was the way her mind worked, assembling connections, decoding histories, and matching linguistic threads across time and place. But lately, there had been interference. Not noise, but feeling. Instincts rise before facts. A flutter in the chest before the thought had time to arrive.

She didn't like it.

Not because she didn't believe in intuition, she did, especially in her mother's kitchen or in the way her maternal grandmother used to read dreams in tea leaves, but because it made her feel unsteady.

And she didn't like being unsteady. Not after the last two years.

Burnout, Ani had said. "You're overdue for stillness."

Which is how she'd ended up in last week's meditation class. It had been fine. Calming. A bit slow. But then... then there'd been a moment.

Not quite a vision. Not quite a dream.

Just this sound....a low, rhythmic chant, not in a language she recognised. And waves. The kind of waves that roll beneath storm clouds. She remembered the feeling more than the images, the pressure behind her eyes, the taste of salt, a voice she both knew and couldn't place.

She hadn't mentioned that part. Not to Ani. Not to anyone.

She paused near the fig tree and sat on the edge of the bench, scarf pulled tighter across her shoulders. Something about the breeze had shifted; cooler, threaded with the scent of early jasmine and the faintest trace of rain, though the sky was clear.

Selena closed her eyes.

A memory stirred, not hers, not entirely. Sand beneath bare feet. Cloth against her cheek. A scroll was pressed into her hand.

Her eyes flew open.

Too fast.

She glanced around, her rising heartbeat. Nothing. Only pigeons. A mother walking with her toddler. A cyclist is weaving along the path.

She reached into her coat pocket and touched the cloth wrap. The seal, nestled inside, felt cool against her fingers.

And then, the streetlamp flickered. Just once. In broad daylight.

A shiver ran down her spine. Not fear. Not quite. But awareness. The same kind she'd felt when her grandmother passed, and every clock in the house stopped for six minutes.

Selena stood. She didn't know what she was feeling, only that it wasn't going away.

And whatever it was, it had begun when she touched that seal.

Fitzroy flat — Late morning

Back in her flat, she unwrapped it again. The terracotta was smooth in some places, and pitted in others. A series of faint symbols curved along the bottom two scripts, side by side. One she thought was Tamil-Brahmi. The other... she wasn't sure yet. Possibly Aramaic. She'd need to send images to someone more familiar with Near Eastern scripts.

But not yet.

Not just yet.

She turned the seal over in her palm. It almost felt warm.

Her breath caught.

For a moment, just a blink, she had the distinct impression that it was watching her.

Perhaps the seal hadn't simply survived the centuries, but perhaps it had been waiting.

Reflections — On the seal, and the sea

Just two days before the coastal visit, she had received confirmation of the new research grant; six months' funding to investigate maritime connections between the Chola empire and the Mediterranean world. The ocean had always carried more than just goods; it ferried myths, language, and people. And somewhere along those ancient routes, between Tamilakam and Alexandria, a seal like this had been pressed into wet clay and passed from one hand to another.

She had spent a life studying artefacts. This one had begun studying her.

Flash Memory — Meditation class, last week

Not quite a vision. Not quite a dream. Just this sound... a low, rhythmic chant, not in a language she recognised. And waves. The kind of waves that roll beneath storm clouds. The pressure behind her eyes. The taste of salt. A voice she both knew and couldn't place.

....

Dream Trace — Edge of memory

A memory stirred, not hers, not entirely. Sand beneath bare feet. Cloth against her cheek. A scroll was pressed into her hand.

....

She had studied artefacts her entire life.
But this one had begun studying her.

Selena's Diary Entry:

Field Notes – Carlton Gardens, Melbourne

Mission:

Investigate the terracotta seal as a Tamil–Aramaic hybrid inscription (est. 1st–2nd century CE) potentially linked to coastal Tamil archive systems; align with newly approved Chola maritime diplomacy study; track the onset of somatic responses and dreams temporally associated with first contact.

Notes (verbatim from field):

Terracotta seal: Tamil–Aramaic hybrid inscription, est. 1st–2nd century CE. Possibly linked to coastal Tamil archive systems. Discovered off Southeast Indian coastline during maritime archaeology survey.

Recent grant approved for Chola maritime diplomacy study.

First tactile reaction: stomach tightens when touched.

Not in fear — in *recognition*.

Smells like fire and ocean, even though it's dry.

Dreams began around the same time I received the seal copy.

Salt, scrolls, serpent coils. And a name I've never spoken in waking life.

Selena's Reflection:

Something's asking to be remembered.

I don't know if I'm ready. But I said yes.

Keywords:

- Chola maritime trade
- Temple-trained female scribes
- "Memory as tidal return"

- Something's asking to be remembered.
- I don't know if I'm ready. But I said yes.

Chapter Three – Scrolls of the Soul

C ollingwood, Melbourne — Late Afternoon (One day earlier)

Before the name climbed bak to the tongue.

Selena hadn't meant to return to the studio. The first time had left her unsettled, not quite frightened, but hesitant in a way she couldn't explain. The hesitation hadn't been helped by the conversation she'd had the day before with Dr Adrian Kerr, a senior academic attached to the Hellenic Maritime Institute, who had offered to "take the seal off her hands for proper cataloguing." His tone had been polite, but barbed. He'd called her theory about Tamil-Aramaic links "ambitious," then "romantic," and finally, "the sort of thing better left to fiction writers."

She hadn't argued. She'd just smiled and felt something harden inside her.

But his voice had followed her home, weaving into her thoughts like a net.

Still, when Ani mentioned another guided meditation in a converted loft in Collingwood, Selena had said yes before she could question it.

Now she sat cross-legged on a mat, late light spilling through a gauzy skylight, turning the room gold and blue. The air was warm, thick with sandalwood and quiet anticipation. Around her, people settled into stillness—some upright and steady, others folded in soft poses of surrender.

The space was bare and deliberate: pale timber floors, a few earthen pots, the hum of the city barely reaching through the glass. At the centre, Soren—the facilitator—stood barefoot beside a single candle. He cupped the flame with practiced grace, and the room fell deeper into silence.

Selena closed her eyes. The wind pressed faintly at the windows.

Soren's voice came low and sure:

"Let the body soften. Let the breath remember. You are not your name. Not your role. Just breathe. Let the tide of memory rise..."

The words floated past her awareness like reeds in water. Her body remained still, but her mind drifted, unmoored.

She felt it first in her stomach, a lurch as if the ground beneath her had tilted. Then came a scent. Brine. Wood. Smoke.

And then the sound, unmistakable, low and rolling waves.

The studio vanished.

....

Dream Trace — Muziris, Malabar Coast, Indian Ocean, Circa 1st Century CE

Dark water stretched in every direction. The sky above was the colour of blue-black ink. The rain had come and gone, leaving the sails heavy and the deck slick. The hull groaned beneath her feet as the vessel cut through the monsoon-tossed sea.

A voice shouted through the storm:

"Vellichi—secure the scrolls!"

She turned instinctively, the name striking through her like a bell.

Not Selena.

Vellichi.

The sound of it settled in her bones as if it had always belonged there.

She stood barefoot, robes damp and clinging at her knees. Her hands were calloused from handling scrolls and salt crates. The scent of frankincense mixed with the sharper tang of fish oil and wet rope. Around her, the murmurs of sailors moved like wind, low, steady, punctuated by occasional laughter or prayers to Varuna between orders.

A deckhand approached, his voice low but urgent over the wind.

"The captain says we'll reach the Nabataean coast by dawn. We'll anchor near Leuke Kome, trade pepper for water, copper, and dates. From there, Berenike, and then Alexandria. You'll deliver your cargo to the temple scribe waiting at the port."

Vellichi nodded, though the words seemed to reach her from underwater.

Alexandria. She'd known it, but hearing it aloud carried weight.

They were three weeks from Muziris, the bustling port on the Malabar Coast where the Periyar River met the Arabian Sea, near what would one day be known as Kerala. Once thick with the scent of pepper, cardamom, and wet timber, Muziris had drawn traders from Alexandria, Antioch, and beyond, all seeking the riches of the East. Now, Vellichi stood aboard a vessel bound westward, the ship laden with scrolls, copper, and secrets. Their next stop would be Berenike, the Egyptian port carved into the Red Sea's desolate rim, a gateway to Alexandria and the Roman world, surrounded by rock, salt winds, and silence. She knew this journey by its rhythms, when to anchor when to hold course, when to trust the ocean's breath more than any map.

But this voyage was not like the others.

She carried something different now.

Beneath the folds of her outer garment, tied close against her skin, was a palm-leaf scroll, bound in red thread and sealed with a coiled serpent pressed in wax. The seal was still warm when it had been handed to her at the sacred jetty, under the gaze of moonlit temple torches.

She hadn't opened it. She didn't need to.

She had known it wasn't hers to read, but only to deliver.

The message was for Alexandria. Perhaps even Rome. But not for her.

And yet, it pulsed against her like a heartbeat.

She steadied herself near the helm, fingers curled around a carved beam slick with rain. The captain gave her a brief nod. He did not ask questions. She travelled under temple protection, which meant she was not to be interfered with. Most thought her a priestess. A few guessed scholars. A trader's widow, perhaps. They would not have been entirely wrong.

But Vellichi had long stopped being explainable in parts.

A call rose from the lookout post. Land to the northwest, the outer markers of the Nabataean coast. There would be another brief anchoring. A cargo swap. Water refills. Possibly messages passed beneath cloaks.

She felt it before she saw him.

A presence. Firm, quiet, known before it had shape.

He stepped aboard not long after. Hooded, cloaked, face obscured by sea-dark cloth. But his stance-tall, poised-sent something ancient rippling through her chest.

She didn't move. Neither did he.

Only when he passed her on the rain-dark deck did he pause for a breath. Not long enough for words. Just long enough for recognition. As he passed, her body stilled. Not from fear, but from something deeper. Recognition, but not just of face or form. A memory that hadn't yet happened. A closeness she hadn't yet earned.

He didn't speak. But somewhere behind the silence, as if it came through water or sleep, she heard it:

"You remembered... too soon."

The words didn't reach her ears. They reached something older.

He knew. And so did she.

No name. No greeting. Only a look; brief, vast, impossible.

Later that night, below deck, she lit a small oil lamp and sat alone. The scroll remained tied, resting against her thigh. She did not open it. Instead, she traced the serpent's imprint with her thumb, the way she once traced chants on a temple wall with sandal paste as a girl.

Some messages are not carried in words.

....

Present Day — Collingwood Studio, Evening

"Selena... begin to come back."

The voice was distant. Gentle. Soft, but pulling.

The waves retreated. The scent of salt faded. Her fingertips tingled as if returning from the frost.

She opened her eyes slowly.

Someone was standing near the stairwell.

Just for a second.

A tall figure, half-shadowed, not part of the group. Dressed in dark grey, hands clasped in front, like he was waiting for someone.

Their eyes met. Hers caught on his, just long enough to freeze her breath.

But then someone moved, and he was gone.

When she looked again, the stairwell was empty.

The skylight above was fogged with condensation. The candle on the floor had guttered. Around her, the room had returned to its still, meditative hush. But her body trembled, not visibly, not outwardly, but deep in the bones, like a bell still ringing beneath the surface.

She touched her lips.

They were dry. Weirdly, it tasted faintly of salt.

She took a breath, and then another. Someone nearby coughed. The world around her reasserted itself, too solid, too sharp.

A name hovered in her mind — round, foreign, familiar.

She mouthed it.

It lingered there, just beneath the tongue. Unspoken. But hers.

Reflections — Between Worlds

Selena hadn't planned to journey this far inward. Yet the trance didn't feel like imagination. It felt like retrieval. The serpent-sealed scroll, the cloaked man, the heartbeat of the sea; all too detailed to dismiss.

And that name. Still unspoken. Still hers.

She woke with salt in her mouth and a name on her lips...
one she had never spoken.

Selena's Diary Entry:
Field Notes – Post-Trance Session
Mission:

Document trance-induced regression. Confirm historical continuity between maritime route visions and Chola–Alexandrian exchange research. Identify symbolic significance of serpent seal and twin-soul figure. Record somatic and emotional responses during meditation sequence.

Meditation induced full-body soul memory. Location: Indian Ocean. Identity: Vellichi ("Velli" in fragments). Role unclear: likely scholar-emissary under temple protection. Carried palm-leaf scroll sealed with serpent emblem.

Emotional Impression:

Grief. Love unspoken. Sacred duty withheld.

Scroll held heat — tangible, not metaphorical.

The cloaked figure — him — was familiar. Too familiar.

Keywords:

- Tamil–Aramaic dual-script scroll
- Chola sea-ambassador lineage
- Twin soul presence = spiritual counterpart
- Memory arrives like the tide — I can't hold it back anymore.

Chapter Four - The Trade Winds Speak

Muscat, Oman — Present Day
The desert wind had a way of scraping silence clean. In Muscat, it slipped through sun-bleached alleyways and along the coral-stone facades of the old port quarter like something ancient, unhurried, and watching. Selena stood outside the Bait Al Zubair Museum, the heat pressing against her skin like a second breath. Behind her, the harbour gleamed blue and endless, the sea she had known in memory and in dream.

This was the gateway.

From ports like Nagapattinam and Puhar, Tamil ships had once sailed west with the monsoon winds, hugging the arc of the Arabian Sea, past the salt mountains of Dhofar, pausing in Sohar and Muscat to unload jars of turmeric and silk, before riding the red winds toward Hormuz and Berenike. Oman had been more than a stop, it had been a threshold. A hinge between two worlds: Indian ritual and Persian mysticism.

She exhaled, then stepped through the museum's carved wooden doors.

Flash Memory — Four Days Earlier, Somewhere over the Indian Ocean
The hum of the aircraft surrounded her like a distant chant. Wrapped in a blanket and lit only by the cold glow of the cabin

window, Selena read over the itinerary Dr Suresh had sent. His note was brief, but loaded with the usual understatement:

"If your seal is genuine, Oman might offer more than context. They've confirmed the coastal registry from Dhofar. Your name's on the grant now. Take it."

She hadn't hesitated long.

The sea had been calling again. And the seal... she couldn't explain it. It wasn't just history anymore. It was personal.

In her satchel, she carried two items: a facsimile of the terracotta seal, and the tiny scroll fragment she'd been cataloguing before the dreams began. On her phone, a voice memo from Ani, calm, grounding, reminding her to stay open.

Now, descending into Muscat, she had the sense of entering not just a new place, but an older version of herself.

Present Day — Bait Al Zubair Museum

The museum was quiet, too early for tour groups, too humid for lingering. She moved past antique khanjars and incense burners, past silver-threaded textiles and coral-dusted relics, until she reached the maritime wing. The exhibit had been curated sparsely: just three low-lit displays and a floor map tracing ancient sea routes.

She stood before a copper urn, greened at the base, flared slightly at the neck. No lid. No inscription.

Yet she knew it.

Her breath hitched.

The placard below read:

Ritual Vessel (unverified)

Provenance: Indian Ocean, est. 1st–2nd century CE

Note: The serpent motif appears in both Tamil and Nabataean ritual iconography. Origin uncertain. Possibly Indo-Persian, pre-Abbasid.

Her fingers brushed the glass. The moment stretched, a breath caught between lifetimes.

The edges of the present blurred.

....

Dream Trace — The Omani Coast, Circa 1st Century CE

She was Vellichi again, or Velli, as her shipmates had called her, not in India, but somewhere west of it, standing at the bow of a cargo ship thick with frankincense and indigo-dyed cloth. The Omani coast shimmered ahead, cliffs rising like teeth from the sea. A flock of ibises lifted from the rocks as the ship neared the inlet. Wind tangled her veil. Her bangles whispered at her wrists.

They docked at nightfall, far from the busy port of Sohar. This was no trade harbour. It was quiet. Hidden. Only two men waited on the stone jetty. One carried a lantern; the other stood in robes of pale grey, lined in black, the hem stitched with a symbol she could not place: a flame within a serpent's mouth.

He said nothing as she approached. He only held out a copper urn, unsealed, yet warm to the touch. Inside, a palm-leaf scroll lay coiled, bound with a cord dyed in temple ash and crushed juniper.

"Who are you?" she asked, her voice quieter than she expected.

His answer came not in words but in a phrase etched into her mind:

"She who seeks fire beneath salt shall find the gate of breath."

From behind a nearby column, a figure watched: Ardeshir, a Persian intermediary merchant, translator, and reluctant agent of empires. He had three daughters at home in Suhar, each one brilliant and bright-tongued, taught in private by their mother. He has been watching Velli, not as a spy. Everytime he watches her, he felt something stir, admiration, envy, a longing he could not name.

"Let my daughters walk the seas as she does," he thought. "Let them be flame-hearted and free."

In Oman, even among the coastal merchant families, daughters were cherished but kept inland.Their futures measured in modest marriages, the success of their sons, and the whispered wisdom they could pass behind closed lattice windows. Few women read outside prayer, fewer still crossed borders with contracts or scrolls. Knowledge lived in their hands, not in their names.

Yet this woman, this Tamil emissary, moved as if no man's permission tethered her breath. She carried knowledge the way some carried weapons: deliberately, with sacred purpose. She spoke softly but with weight, as though ritual and diplomacy flowed from the same source. And she had not lost her grace, her veils, her scent, the click of her bangles. She was still a woman, entirely. Not hardened, not hidden. Just *whole*.

Ardeshir felt it rise in him, not just envy, but grief for what his own daughters would be denied. And wonder for what empires, like hers, must have once dared to become.

She turned her head slightly, and for a moment, their eyes met, a silent acknowledgement between witness and myth.

Then the world collapsed into light.

....

Museum Awakening – Present Day

Selena staggered back from the display case, heart hammering. Her palm tingled where it had hovered above the glass. She blinked, sweat gathering at the base of her neck.

She didn't know how long she'd been standing there.

The museum guard gave her a curious look as he passed. She nodded faintly, the spell still clinging.

She pulled out her notebook and scribbled the phrase as best she could remember it. Beneath it, she wrote a single question:

"Where is the gate of breath?"

Museum Corridor & Muttrah Corniche – Present Day

"Dr Ravenscroft?"

The voice broke gently through the air. She turned to see a tall Omani woman in a pale linen blouse and navy trousers. Her dark curls were neatly tied back, her expression composed but warm.

"Samira Al-Kharusi," she said, offering her hand. "I'm your research liaison from the Ministry. I believe we're headed to Dhofar together?"

Selena smiled, grateful, still shaken. "Yes. I've just had... an intense moment."

Samira raised an eyebrow, then nodded. "Oman has a habit of remembering things before we do."

They walked together through the corridor, past exhibits and maps, past the long arc of history etched in spice and sea.

Samira Al-Kharusi had the bearing of someone born to desert wind and ink. Her scarf was loosely draped, cream cotton stitched with rust-red palm motifs. Her skin held the deep bronze of mountain sun, and her eyes were lined with quiet precision, dark, almond-shaped, always reading. She carried a satchel heavy with local dialect studies and excavation notes, and wore her authority without apology.

When Selena met her at the museum steps that evening, the woman didn't extend a hand but greeted her with a nod that felt like it had weight.

"You've walked through thresholds before, haven't you?" Samira said by way of introduction.

Selena blinked. "I... suppose I have."

"Good. The desert doesn't like tourists. It remembers seekers."

Over dinner at a small outdoor restaurant near Muttrah Corniche, they sat at a table ringed with lanterns, the sea breeze tangling through copper bowls of grilled fish and saffron rice.

Samira poured thick Arabic coffee into tiny cups and leaned forward. "I've read your work. Your eyes don't match your methods. You write like a scholar, but your field notes read like someone listening to ghosts."

Selena smiled, caught off guard. "Is that criticism or admiration?"

"Neither. Just recognition." Samira's voice dropped lower. "This place.... Oman .... it remembers older things. Trade, yes, but also transmission. It's not just goods that crossed the sea. It was prayer, vision, ritual. Scrolls."

Selena felt the seal pulse in her memory.

Samira tilted her head. "What did you bring with you?"

Selena hesitated. "A name I don't understand. And a memory I haven't earned yet."

"Then you'll fit right in." Samira lifted her cup. "To the sea and what it still carries."

They drank in silence. Not awkward, just full. Something between them had settled already. Like two winds from different coasts finally meeting on open water.

Reflections — Hotel Room, Late Night

That night, Selena sat cross-legged on the tiled floor of her hotel room, the fan ticking overhead like an old clock. Her laptop pinged, an email from Dr Suresh.

Subject: Fragment from Dhofar

Body: "You'll want to see this. May be nothing. Or everything."

The attachment loaded slowly, a photo of a stone fragment carved with a partial inscription in Tamil-Brahmi script. One line, eroded but legible, caught her eye:

"...to the monastery of ash and wind..."

She read it three times. Her throat tightened.

A wind rose suddenly outside the window, dry and salt-heavy. It struck the shutters once, then died. The hotel lights flickered. Somewhere in the distance, a call to prayer rang out, slow and sonorous, like an echo returned from the sea.

Selena lowered her head into her hands.

She hadn't come to Oman seeking refuge.

But the land was already remembering her arrival.

*She wasn't sure what she was remembering,
only that it was remembering her too.*

Selena's Diary Entry:
Field Notes – Muscat / Bait Al Zubair Museum
Mission:

To trace the threshold between sea and desert — where Tamil temple rites met Persian mysticism.

To decode the phrase *"She who seeks fire beneath salt shall find the gate of breath."*

To identify the monastery of ash and wind referenced in the Dhofar fragment and understand its connection to the serpent-flame lineage.

To discern why Oman feels less like discovery and more like return.

Object:

Copper ritual urn, possibly Tamil–Nabataean origin. No formal provenance. Appears in trance-memory sequence as handed over by cloaked man with Zoroastrian-Sufi symbols.

Historical pattern:

Chola–Persian maritime threshold. Oman as knowledge hinge between temple and desert mystic.

Phrase heard:

"She who seeks fire beneath salt shall find the gate of breath."

It followed me out of trance. I wrote it three times. My hand was shaking.

Keywords:

- Sacred sea lanes
- Zoroastrian monasteries (off-grid)
- Samira – local contact. Quiet. Watching. I think she's remembering too.

- Vessel = scroll = me?

Chapter Five – The Twin Flame Divide

Stone Town, Zanzibar — Present Day

Two days ago, she had left Oman under a restless sky. The scent of sea salt and myrrh still clung to her scarf. From the window seat of the plane, she had watched the coast unravel, mountains to sea to memory. The historic Muscat–Zanzibar route had once carried cinnamon, pearls, and sacred cargo. Now it carried her, and something she couldn't yet name. A short connecting flight through Nairobi, and now she was here, on the island whose salt still whispered of Tamil sails and Arab gold.

Zanzibar's air carried secrets. Not the whispered kind, but those too ancient to speak, folded deep into coral-stone walls and salted timber beams, into the scent of clove and sea that drifted through the city like breath.

Selena stood at the edge of Stone Town's old harbour, a linen scarf pressed to her neck, watching the tide shift around the anchored dhows. Sunlight danced across the hulls like something alive. The sound of prayer had just ebbed from the minarets behind her, and now only the wind and gulls remained.

She had been in Zanzibar three days now, long enough for the air to feel familiar, and for the tide inside her to shift again.

Officially, she was here following a trail; a series of maritime Tamil inscriptions recorded by a Swahili antiquities collective. Unofficially, she was chasing a feeling. The pull that had started in Melbourne, deepened in Muscat, and now whispered louder with each sunrise.

Beit el-Ajaib Archives — Afternoon
It hadn't taken long to find something that unsettled her.

At the Beit el-Ajaib archives, the House of Wonders, a faded vellum scroll sat tucked behind weathered manuscripts and trade manifests. Written in Tamil-Brahmi and half-erased by humidity, it referenced a Chola woman-poet, revered for sea rites performed at a coastal shrine. Her title was uncertain. Her name, partial:

"Ma... yi... lai."

The rest was torn.

Selena's throat tightened. That name. The syllables had come to her before, through dreams, through salt.

The archivist, a kind-eyed Swahili scholar named Jabari, offered her black coffee laced with clove as they read the fragment aloud together. "Many Tamil traders were here," he said, pointing to a mural of saffron-robed men on the port wall. "But this..." he tapped the scroll, "this speaks of a woman not just trading, but invoking. Offering. That was rare."

Stone Town Streets — Evening
With the light softening into ochre, Selena wandered through the narrow lanes of Stone Town, the elaborately carved doorways, reminders of a Seahili world shaped by Persian, Arab, Indian, and Portugese hands, pressing in like watchful eyes. The streets of Stone Town curled like old script, sun-bleached and heavy with memory. Sandstone walls leaned

inwards, whispering secrets of the past, spices clung to the air, cloves, cardamom, drying seaweed, while above her, faded balconies spilled with bougainvillea, laundry, and cats napping like royalty.

Selena had walked that morning past the old Omani Fort, where cannons once faced the harbour, and the House of Wonders once the first building in East Africa to have electricity and a lift, now a shell of faded grandeur. The scent of spices rose from every market stall, carried by sea winds that had once borne silk and song from Tamil shores.It was a city that never fully belonged to the present, always half in ceremony, half in forgetting. And today, it felt as if the tide of something long buried was rising again.

She turned off a side alley and entered the shrine ruins near Kiponda, a space now more stone than sanctuary. But the energy still held. It was there, between the coral bricks and fig roots, in the silence that wrapped her.

By evening, something inside her grew restless. She skipped dinner, returned to her room, and lit the travel candle she kept wrapped in her scarf.

Sandalwood. Flame. Breath.

She hadn't planned to meditate that night, not here, not with so much rawness still under her skin. But the ache behind her ribs had begun to whisper again. It wasn't just longing. It was calling.

She sat cross-legged on the woven mat, hands open, breath slowing. A hum rose in her chest, familiar now. Almost welcome.

She didn't call the vision.

It came anyway.

Dream Trace — Zanzibar Coast, Circa 1st Century CE

Salt. Wind. Fire.

She stood at the steps of a sea shrine carved from black stone and coral reef. Velli, as the men who feared her power called her, wore indigo robes edged in copper, her bangles singing softly with each movement. A garland of dried lotus wound through her braided hair. The air was thick with myrrh and tide.

Twelve acolytes stood in a circle. At the centre, a basin of seawater shimmered beneath moonlight. She stepped forward, unfastening the serpent-bound pouch at her hip.

In her hands, a coiled palm-leaf scroll pulsed, not with magic, but memory. She whispered over it, calling no deity by name, only the truth of the tide.

A presence stirred behind her.

She didn't turn. She knew the weight of his silence.

He stepped forward slowly, his feet bare, robe rain-dark and frayed at the hem. The hood stayed drawn, but his energy folded around her like warmth long missed. Her breath caught, not from fear, but from recognition.

"You came," she said.

"As I always do," he replied, voice low, sand-worn.

She held out the scroll.

He did not take it.

"This is not yet ours to keep," he said. "Only to carry."

Their fingers brushed. The scroll passed between them, not as lovers, but as flame-bearers.

They were not to touch.

Not in this life.

"Will it always be like this?" she asked, her voice breaking. "Finding. Losing. Remembering too late?"

He looked toward the sea.

"Until the world is ready. Until we are."

He turned to go. She stepped forward, but the space between them held. She couldn't cross it.

Not yet.

His face was never revealed. Only the outline.

Only the ache.

....

Reflections — Night, Stone Town

Selena woke gasping. Her face was wet, either from sweat or tears, or both. The room was dark, but not cold. Her body pulsed like it had been singing for hours. Her hands trembled in her lap, still shaped to the scroll she no longer held.

She whispered aloud, though no one was there to hear her: "He knew me. But he left."

The words broke as they landed.

She touched her lips. There had been no kiss, no touch, and still, she felt more hollow than if he'd held her and let her go. What was this pain, carried across time? A wound or a vow?

The distant call to prayer from the Malindi Mosque drifted in waves. Nearby, the bustle of Darajani Market was beginning to swell, merchants shouting prices over mounds of cinnamon, dried fish, and saffron. The world had returned. But she hadn't fully come back with it.

She rose and went to the desk, still barefoot. In the notebook, with shaking hands, she wrote the phrase from the dream, the words he had spoken:

"Only to carry."

She didn't understand it. Not entirely.

But her heart did.

The tightness inside her wasn't grief, it was recognition. It was from the old knowing, that some loves burn not to warm, but to *remind*.

To promise.

Her phone vibrated once on the floor beside her bed. A voice note from Samira.

"Selena... just checking in. I had the strangest dream last night. Something about salt and snakes. No idea why, but I thought of you. I know this sounds mad, but do you think dreams can echo each other?"

Selena stared at the screen, the message playing again in her mind.

Salt. Snakes. Dreams.

The tide was pulling them both now.

Outside her window, the night sea whispered against the ancient stone. Somewhere across the water, memory moved like a tide waiting for the next moon.

They had found each other again and walked away, again.
And still, the sea remembered what the world could not.

Selena's Diary Entry:

Field Notes – Zanzibar / Kiponda Shrine Ruins

Mission:

To uncover the Chola–Swahili connection through the poet-priestess Mayilai.

To understand the nature of the vow: *Only to carry.*

To trace the spiritual function of twin flames not as lovers, but as bearers of sacred continuity.

To determine if the Kiponda shrine aligns with the "monastery of ash and wind" mentioned in the Dhofar fragment.

Findings:

Beit el-Ajaib scroll fragment: Chola woman-poet invoked sea rites at Swahili coast shrine. Name mostly torn: Ma... yi... lai.

Trance-memory:

Mayi conducts sea offering with twelve acolytes, passes scroll to cloaked soul twin. They do not touch. They do not speak of love.

Phrase repeated:

"Only to carry."

Selena's reflection:

He knew me. And walked away again.

It was duty, not rejection. But it hurts like both.

Samira dreamt of salt and snakes. That can't be a coincidence.

Keywords:

- Chola–Swahili trade arc
- Sacred poetry

- Twin flame as a spiritual task
- This isn't romance. This is resurrection.

Chapter Six - The Falcon's Gate

Dubai — Present Day

D The falcon arrived before the questions did.

Selena spotted it from the airport shuttle as she passed through the glass corridors of Dubai International, perched atop a tall Emirates banner, wings outstretched, eyes unblinking. She wasn't sure why it made her breath catch. Perhaps it was nothing. Perhaps it was everything.

By the time she reached her hotel room overlooking the glittering downtown skyline, the falcon was waiting again, this time carved into the brass doorknob of the suite. A motif, she told herself, maybe a coincidence. But the way her hand trembled as she turned the handle said otherwise.

She was in Dubai for a two-day academic conference on intercultural maritime diplomacy. Her paper was meant to be dry: Tamil naval routes, the politics of multilingual seals, early women emissaries. But beneath the structure of her talk, her soul churned like a tide mid-storm. She hadn't come for slides. She had come for the pull.

Dubai was a city that shimmered, but never settled. It was all edge and height, towers that kissed the clouds, malls that mimicked Venice and Cairo in one breath, fountains that danced to pop songs. Everything gleamed, and yet nothing seemed to breathe. To Selena, it felt like walking through a high-gloss dream made of steel and thirst.

She admired its ambition, but not its soul. The crowds overwhelmed her, and the neon promises felt too loud. Beneath every glass ceiling was a hum of something hungry. It was a city drunk on becoming.

And she, lately, was learning to unbecome.

Muscat Connection — Late Night

On the second evening, she skipped the final panel. Instead, she opened her tablet and stared again at the annotated map Samira had sent from Muscat. Al-Balid, near Salalah. Dhofar coast. An ancient trading city. Falcon seals had been found etched into coral-brick foundations and stored in the back archives of the local museum.

Samira's note was brief: "Something about this felt right. Could be nothing. Or not. —S."

That night, Selena booked a last-minute flight to Salalah, deep in Oman's southern crescent, once a hub of frankincense trade and Tamil maritime diplomacy. She told no one. Not even Leila, the one friend who kept her anchored to the ordinary when the world started to tilt.

Dhofar, Southern Oman — Arrival

Dhofar was nothing like Dubai. Here, the air had weight, not just of salt and heat, but of memory. Long before sky towers and artificial islands, this land had been a maritime hinge, where Indian, Persian, African, and Arab trade routes converged in silent agreement.

In its glory days, the port of Al-Balid had thrived as the crown jewel of the frankincense trade. It was the scent of empire, burned in temples from Alexandria to Kyoto, carried in carved teak boxes by Tamil merchants who navigated the monsoon winds with only stars and instinct. Dhofar wasn't just part of the Naval Silk Road. It was the breath of it.

Ships once arrived here heavy with cinnamon, sandalwood, and Chinese porcelain. They left stained with incense, pearls, and secrets. Zafar, the old name of the city, had even found mention in Greco-Roman maps, described as a place of 'sweet smoke and cloudless sky.'

But nothing lasts.

By the 16th century, Portuguese cannons had redrawn coastlines, and desert winds slowly swallowed the old port stones. Now, Al-Balid's ruins crouched beneath wild grasses and storm-heavy skies, half-forgotten, a hymn that no longer had singers.

Selena felt it before she saw it: the sense of arrival not just in space, but in time. This wasn't history. This was recognition.

When Selena arrived at the conservation gate, the sky was swollen with pre-monsoon cloud. There was a hush in the wind, the kind that presses against skin like a question.

She signed in at the conservation tent and was met by a local guide, someone Samira had arranged in advance.

He introduced himself with a hand to his chest. "I am Farid ibn Kamal, son of a fisherman, former archaeology student... now your lucky bodyguard-slash-research escort."

Selena smiled. "I've been called worse."

He gestured ahead. "You're not here for the tourist section, are you?"

She shook her head. "I'm here for what isn't on the map."

Farid nodded slowly. "Then you've come to the right ruins."

They walked together through stone foundations and coral-brick walls, half-swallowed by sand and time. The air was thick with salt, frankincense, and dry thyme. Beneath her boots, the soil felt unsettled, like a breath waiting to be exhaled.

They paused at a roped-off excavation zone. Farid crouched and gently brushed dust from a stone block.

There, faint but clear, was the outline of a falcon, wings drawn inward, beak open mid-cry.

Selena's breath caught. "That's it."

Farid glanced at her. "What is?"

She crouched beside him, fingers hovering, reverent. "I've seen this before. Or something like it."

Farid didn't press. He scanned the horizon. "I'll give you space," he said gently. "But be careful. These ruins are older than memory sometimes."

Selena knelt, eyes locked on the seal.

The falcon watched her.

And then, the trance came.

....

Dream Trace — Strait of Hormuz, Circa 11th Century CE

She was at sea.

Not drifting, but slicing through the Strait of Hormuz like a blade through silk. The vessel beneath her was Chola-built, lean and low, modified for speed and stealth. No flags. No temple markers. Just wood dark with brine, and men who thought they were carrying a gift, not a weapon.

She was Mayilai again. But this was not the ritualist of Zanzibar's rites. This Mayi moved like a shadow among whispers. Her veil was silk, her posture deferent, but her spine held fire.

To the crew, she was cargo. A learned courtesan for a Hormuz noble. She let them believe it.

Beneath the drape of her robe, tucked against her side, pulsed a scroll sealed in jade-green wax. Etched upon it: a falcon in profile, wings drawn inward, claws poised mid-flight. It was not the roaring tiger of conquest, nor the ceremonial elephant used in Chola treaty scrolls. The falcon was rarer still reserved for spiritual missions, esoteric alliances, and sacred codes carried only by those trusted to walk between worlds. It was the private seal of Rajendra Chola I, Emperor of the Southern Oceans.

This wasn't a message of politics. It was a vow.

Not a role she played. A contract her soul had chosen, long ago.

The temple elder who entrusted her with the scroll had said:

"This message is not for kings. It's for the firekeepers. You are the flame they forgot."

The wind grew restless.

A storm had begun to stir. Salt lashed the deck. Sailors shouted, their voices sharp with fear.

One pointed at her. "You! Woman! Down!"

She didn't move.

Instead, she stepped forward, toward the prow of the ship. Rain tangled in her hair. Her veil slipped. Her face met the wind, not as defiance, but recognition.

In that moment, something ancient clicked into place.

A fire low in her belly stirred, Sacral Chakra, where creation and purpose awaken.

A tightening, then expansion at her solar plexus, the center of identity and will.

Her soul contract was activating.

Not memory. Not story.

A mission. Rekindled.

The sea began to calm. The storm blinked back.

The ship stilled.

The scroll at her side seemed to warm, as though acknowledging its moment.

And then, a voice.

Close. Familiar. Cloaked in wind.

"You remembered too soon."

She turned.

A silhouette stood near the mast, robed, unseen, and somehow known. The one who always appeared at the edge of each life.

But before she could speak, the vision folded.

The salt became air. The ship became sand. The falcon became stone.

....

Flash Memory — The Gate Within

Her breath hitched. The falcon's eye gleamed like molten gold. A single image flashed; a monastery carved into white cliffs, wind howling through arched corridors, a symbol of flame inside a serpent's mouth. Then it was gone.

Reflections — Al-Balid Ruins, Twilight

Selena gasped, back on her knees, the stone seal before her.

Her hands trembled. The sand beneath her was damp with sweat.

Farid returned with a bottle of water, kneeling beside her. "Are you alright?"

She nodded slowly. "No. But also yes."

He didn't press. But something softened behind his eyes, a quiet understanding, shaped by things not spoken.

They walked silently back toward the car.

As they passed beneath the last arch of the ruined port city, the wind stirred again. Selena stopped, eyes closing.

She whispered under her breath:

"You cannot pass through until the self dies."

She didn't know who had said it.

But now, it lived in her bones.

The gate she feared to open was already ajar.

Selena's Diary Entry:

Field Notes – Zanzibar / Kiponda Shrine Ruins

Mission:

To trace the falcon seal as the emblem of sacred diplomacy within Chola maritime networks.

To uncover its link to Rajendra Chola I's esoteric emissaries — the "firekeepers."

To locate the monastery of ash and wind hinted at through trance.

To understand what "You cannot pass through until the self dies" means in spiritual and psychological terms.

Findings:

Dream sequence: Mayilai sails through the Strait of Hormuz disguised as a courtesan-scholar, carrying a jade-sealed falcon scroll.

Falcon seal distinct from royal emblems — represents spiritual alliance, not conquest.

Phrase and imagery suggest passage rites — "Gate of Breath" tied to self-transcendence.

Phrase repeated:

"You cannot pass through until the self dies."

Selena's reflection:

This isn't about history anymore — not the kind that fits into a thesis.

I carried something ancient across the Strait, disguised, silent, burning.

This time, his distance felt like instruction, not punishment.

Keywords:

- Al-Balid ruins
- Rajendra Chola I's emblem system
- Falcon = spiritual/diplomatic seal
- Zoroastrian/Sufi monastery threads
- Twin soul resistance / spiritual threshold
- Ego death as initiation

Chapter Seven - The Mirror of Pearls

George Town, Penang, Malaysia — Present Day

Selena hadn't planned on Penang. Not until a message from Professor Samira landed in her inbox two nights after Dhofar. The subject line had simply read: "Chola–Srivijaya traces in Penang – urgent lead?" Attached were high-resolution scans of a Tamil-Brahmi inscription found embedded in a temple wall during a cultural restoration walk. Alongside them, a local exhibition flyer: "Maritime Mirrors: Tamil and Austronesian Echoes."

Samira's note was characteristically terse:

"Might be nothing. But something about the pearl motifs and falcon symbols matches what you described from Salalah. Also, local oral stories link these carvings to a Tamil emissary who 'walked across rain into a golden city.' Worth chasing?"

Selena had booked a flight the next morning. Salalah to Muscat, Muscat to Kuala Lumpur, then on to Penang. Three layovers, no hesitation. The pull had returned, sharp as salt and memory. If Oman had offered her a gateway, Penang felt like the next threshold.

Transit – Between Salalah and Kuala Lumpur

The flight from Salalah to Muscat was uneventful, but the long journey east gave Selena space and solitude. In the liminal hours between airports, she reread her notes, sipped weak coffee at gate lounges in Doha and Kuala Lumpur, and fell into quiet trances on long-haul flights. Somewhere above the Indian Ocean, she sat quietly against the cabin wall near the back, earbuds in, but no music playing, just her breath, syncing with the hum of the engines.

Between flights, she answered emails and messages.

A short voice note from Soren:

"Selena, you're not losing your mind. Visions come when the body is ready, not the mind. Keep grounding. Keep breathing. I'm here."

A WhatsApp text from Ani blinked in at 2:11 a.m. Melbourne time:

"I had a dream you were standing on a ship, covered in rain, looking for someone. You okay?"

Selena replied:

"Same ship. I think we're both remembering something. Will call you from Penang."

She hesitated, then pressed the call icon despite still at Kuala Lumpur International Airport.

The line clicked, soft static between continents.

Ani: "You sound... far away."

Selena (smiling faintly): "I am. Physically and otherwise."

Ani: "Your message freaked me out a bit. The dream felt so real. You were soaked, calling a name I couldn't hear. And then the sea swallowed the sound."

Selena: "It's strange you said that. I've been dreaming of ships, seals, names that feel like déjà vu."

Ani: "Do you think it's stress?"

Selena: "Maybe. Or maybe memory doesn't always belong to one lifetime."

Ani (gentle pause): "Just promise me you'll keep one foot in this world, okay? You've got a habit of floating between them."

Selena (soft laugh): "I'll try. But the tide's strong lately."

Ani: "Then tie yourself to something that matters. Even if it's just me nagging you from Melbourne."

Selena (quietly): "That's what keeps me anchored."

The boarding announcement cut through her earbuds.

Ani: "Go. Call me when you land."

Selena: "I will."

The line went silent, but the warmth lingered like an ember; a reminder that not all connections needed reincarnation to endure.

George Town, Penang — Evening Arrival

The flight descended through cloudbursts, the island below unfolding like a mosaic of light and water. Penang International Airport shimmered under a film of tropical rain, its glass façade reflecting the runway lights like liquid silver. Beyond the tarmac, palms bowed toward the sea, their silhouettes caught between storm and sunset.

Inside the arrival hall, the air was thick with spice and humid; a warmth that didn't just cling to skin but to memory itself. Signboards in Malay, Tamil, Chinese, and English glowed side by side; four languages breathing in unison. Selena smiled, port cities always reminded her that civilisation was less about conquest than coexistence.

As she passed the visitor displays near the baggage hall, a small exhibition caught her eye, University Science Malaysia:

Fifty Years of Discovery. Photographs of coral restoration, maritime archaeology, and cultural heritage projects filled the glass panels. One image showed students studying temple fragments along Kedah's coast, another, a team analysing Chola-era ceramics found off Langkawi.

Selena slowed, reading the captions with quiet admiration.

"Even here," she murmured, "the sea keeps teaching."

The memory of Dhofar pressed faintly at the edges of her mind, the falcon, the monastery, the vow. Somehow, Penang didn't feel like a new destination. It felt like the next chapter of the same lesson.

Outside, the taxi queue shimmered under fluorescent light. She handed her bags to the driver and settled into the back seat. The road from Bayan Lepas curved along coastal inlets where fishing boats rocked under a bruised purple sky.

The driver, a soft-spoken man with silver hair and a Tottenham Hotspurs sticker on his dashboard, glanced at her in the mirror.

"First time in Penang, miss?"

Selena smiled faintly. "First time in this life, maybe."

He laughed, not unkindly. "That's how this island works. It remembers everyone."

They passed the sprawling USM campus on the hill; a sweep of trees and amber lights scattered through the rain. The main archway read University Science Malaysia – Engineering the Future, Preserving the Past. The phrase lingered with her. It was almost what she herself had been trying to do.

When the car turned into Leith Street, the city tightened into its colonial heart; pastel shophouses shoulder to shoulder with old mansions and half-forgotten shrines. The driver stopped before a whitewashed façade crowned with wrought-iron balconies: The Edison George Town.

The lobby smelled faintly of lemongrass and teak. Ceiling fans turned lazily above a mosaic floor in blue and pearl. Old black-and-white photographs lined the walls; Tamil sailors, Chinese merchants, Arab spice traders, mid-gesture, mid-bargain, mid-life.

As the concierge handed her a brass room key, Selena noticed the pattern engraved on it, two interlocking spirals. Her pulse caught. She'd seen that pattern before, stitched into Mayilai's sari in a dream.

In her room, the shutters opened onto Muntri Street, the cobblestones slick with rain. The air smelled of clove, jasmine, and the faint sweetness of street mangoes.

"Home," she whispered, though she wasn't sure which century she meant.

Somewhere beyond the rooftops, a temple bell rang, not loud, but certain, as if it had been waiting for her.

That evening, she met her local contact, Meera Madhavan, a Tamil-Malaysian historian who had worked on the temple conservation project. Warm, effortlessly funny, and sharp-eyed, Meera reminded Selena of her cousin from Brisbane. They bonded easily over local milk tea, teh tarik, and shared exhaustion.

Over dinner at Fire by Shankar, a tucked-away South Indian restaurant lit by hanging lanterns and the constant shuffle of dosa griddles, Meera introduced her to the rhythm of Penang:

"You can't understand our history without understanding our food," Meera said, tearing into a fluffy appam. "The Tamil influence is in every sambhar bowl here, but it's stitched into memory, not textbooks."

Selena tasted crisp masala vadai (spices infused indian donut), tamarind-rich meen kuzhambu (fish curry), and her new favourite, banana leaf thali served with smoky eggplant curry, mango pickle, and rasam (indian soup) that seared through jetlag like incense. Over fiery chettinad mutton, they spoke of empire and erasure, the old ways hidden in temple lintels and family recipes. All the food went well with a diluted yoghurt drink, not lassi, which was much thinner, called mooru. Selena had some room left in her tummy, which was already filled up with all the delicacies, for thairee vadai (indian donut soaked in temper yoghurt)

"You're not just chasing history," Meera observed, pouring more ginger tea. "You're remembering something, aren't you?"

Selena blinked.

"Is it that obvious?"

"Only to someone who's seen it too."

Later that night, back in her hotel room, Selena lit a stick of sandalwood incense, sat at the foot of the bed, and whispered a mantra she didn't know she remembered. She didn't need the map anymore. The pull was alive inside her bones.

Sri Mahamariamman Temple — Pre-Dawn

They agreed to meet at the Sri Mahamariamman Temple at dawn, a quiet time, before the tourist footfall, before the drums.

The old stones hummed beneath her fingers.

Selena knelt before the weathered Tamil carving on the outer wall of the Sri Mahamariamman Temple in George Town, Penang. The stone was porous, rain-softened by two centuries of tropical storms, but the figure remained, a goddess with four arms, hips swaying like a dancer, one palm raised in a gesture of benediction. At her feet, a line of script: ancient, sharp, unmistakably Tamil-Brahmi.

She wasn't supposed to be here. The cultural exhibition had ended hours ago. Her press pass still hung around her neck, swaying gently in the humid night air. The incense from the temple lingered with jasmine and salt, the kind of salt that didn't come from tears, but from sea memory.

A guide earlier had mentioned the stone was likely older than the temple itself. Brought from a ruin near Langkawi, it had been placed here in reverence.

Selena found a quiet corner inside the temple, tucked between an unlit brass oil lamp and a pillar draped in saffron cloth. She folded into a seated posture, cross-legged on the stone floor. Closing her eyes, she let her palms rest gently on her knees, thumbs touching forefingers, the mudra of stability.

Soren's voice came to her memory like a breeze across incense:

"Begin with the root. Feel the base of your spine sink into the earth. You're not floating through time, Selena. You're planted. That's where the remembering begins."

She drew her breath low and deep. Down past her lungs, down into the pelvis, down into the earth. Visualising a warm, ember-red light at the base of her spine, the root chakra, or Muladhara, she inhaled slowly and released.

The vibration of the temple, the ancient stone, the whisper of rituals long past, they all began to rise and harmonise with her field. The pulse of Penang. The memory of empire. It wasn't imagination. It was resonance.

She wasn't just grounding into her body.

She was anchoring into time.

....

Dream Trace — Srivijaya, Circa 11th Century CE

She was no longer seated in a temple in Penang.

She stood barefoot on a slick stone dock, the sky above her bloated with monsoon clouds. Rain blurred the torchlight, but the tide held stillness, like the world had paused to watch. Behind her, the great Chola vessel that had carried her across the Bay of Bengal creaked against its mooring. Ahead: the Srivijayan port city, a jewel carved into the green, smoke-laced cliffs. Somewhere beyond the fog, a temple bell rang.

She was Mayilai again, Mayi, emissary of Rajendra Chola I, chosen not only for her literacy in court dialects, but for her understanding of the codes women spoke beneath their words. Her sari was wet through, but still held the sacred pattern stitched into its border: interlocking pearls and twin spirals, the signal for sacred delivery.

Two generals had accompanied her to Sumatra's shores. Both remained aboard, per custom. This was not a military show. This was diplomacy, wrapped in ritual.

She adjusted her copper bangles, still cold from the sea, and stepped into the rain.

The court that was waiting for her was smaller than expected. No royal procession. No lavish welcome. Only a few Srivijayan monks in saffron robes, a single court scribe, and a man cloaked in deep indigo, face half-veiled, the mark of a trusted intermediary.

Her breath hitched, but she didn't falter. Not here.

A female attendant stepped forward and placed a garland of frangipani around Mayi's neck. No words. Just a small nod. The welcome was symbolic, not warm, but wary. Tensions still simmered after Rajendra Chola's strike along Srivijaya's coast. The Cholas had burned, conquered, and then offered peace, an unusual, generous peace by placing Tamil generals in Srivijayan courts. Not to rule, but to protect sea routes from further disruption.

Those generals, they said, had married Srivijayan princesses, a custom most common in those days to ensure a strong alliance with the locals under the watchful eye of ones own empire. Their descendants would later found cities, alliances, and even new kingdoms. One, it was whispered, would one day birth Malacca itself.

But this was not history yet. This was Mayi's now.

She walked the steps into the port shrine, not the royal palace and placed the scroll she carried on the altar beside a bowl of pearls and sandalwood. The scroll bore a falcon seal, flanked by twin serpents. The symbol of silent pacts. Used only in high orders, knowledge between priestesses and commanders, not meant for men to interpret.

She bowed.

The cloaked intermediary approached. No name. No greeting. No titles.

"The seal is received," he said, bowing low.

Mayilai bowed back.

The exchange was not just political. It was ancestral.

"You carry a code," he added, "that has not been spoken since the last flood."

"It lives in the pearls," she replied.

"Then it will outlive us both."

....

Armenian Street, Late Evening - Present Day

The rain had thinned to a mist by the time Selena and Meera stepped out of the temple.

As they walked toward Armenian Street, the murals seemed to turn toward her; children on bicycles, gods in motion, eyes that followed from painted walls.

Selena felt as though the city itself was alive, breathing her name in slow exhalations of rain and incense.

Her phone buzzed.

A new message from the Penang State Museum:

"Ms. Ravenscroft, we've located a second inscription stone from Langkawi. Matches the Penang piece. Would you like to view it?"

She read it twice. Then a third time.

Her pulse didn't quicken; it steadied, a quiet recognition more than surprise. Langkawi. The island of drowned myths and whispered penance. She remembered stories of Mahsuri, the woman cursed to bleed white, purity punished, truth buried alive.

Every empire had a Mahsuri, she thought. Every truth, a tomb.

She stared at the message again. The phrasing struck her.

Would you like to view it?

It wasn't a question. It felt like a summons.

Through the shifting reflections on her phone screen, she caught the faint glimmer of lightning far across the straits, the direction of Langkawi.

A storm was forming there.

A memory surfaced, a phrase she'd once read in her father's old field notes from Tamil Nadu:

"When two stones speak, a gate remembers."

She closed her eyes.

Two stones.

Two scripts.

Two lives.

"Are you alright?" Meera asked softly.

Selena nodded, still watching the dark horizon.

"I think the next piece just surfaced."

"Langkawi?"

"Yes."

Meera exhaled, a small smile forming. "That island keeps its secrets well. Maybe it's time one of us asked the right questions."

Selena slipped the phone into her pants pocket, the weight of it like a heartbeat.

Outside, thunder rolled faintly, not loud, but deliberate, the sound of the sea remembering.

She looked toward the water and whispered,

"Yes. I'm listening."

Reflections — Penang Departure

The next morning, as dawn bled gold across the Strait, Selena stood by the window of her hotel, tracing the outline of the horizon with her fingertip.

She could almost see it; the misty line where Penang's coast blurred into the distant silhouette of Langkawi.

History wasn't finished speaking.

It was only changing language.

Peace had been brokered that day not with words,
but with silence, veils, and pearls.

Selena's Diary Entry
Field Notes – George Town, Penang
Mission:
To investigate Tamil-Brahmi inscription at Sri Mahamariamman Temple and determine connection to Srivijaya–Chola diplomatic exchanges.

Temple meditation triggered a full trance recalling the Pearl Pact — Mayilai's role as spiritual envoy in Srivijaya.

Phrase repeated: "Do you still carry the fire?"
Phrase Repeated:
"Do you still carry the fire?"

Selena's Reflection:
Mayilai walked into Srivijaya not as a conqueror, but as a keeper of balance.

The twin soul was there again. Unnamed. Cloaked.

The fire between them didn't burn out. It waited.

There was no war between them. Only recognition.

Now Langkawi calls.

When two stones speak, a gate remembers.

Chakra Thread:
Root → Sacral → Solar — grounding memory into creative purpose and identity rebirth.

Keywords:

- Chola–Srivijaya naval diplomacy
- Karmic diplomacy
- Root Chakra activation
- Ancestral codes via pearls
- Veiled emissary / feminine power

- Founding of Malacca (linked via Tamil–Srivijaya lineage)
- Langkawi inscription mirror
- Emotional compass as soul map

Chapter Eight – The Island Remembers

Langkawi, Kedah – Present Day

The ferry eased away from Penang's jetty with a groan of metal and a sigh of sea. Selena claimed a window seat near the stern, where spray from the Andaman Sea caught her face like a benediction. The morning light was liquid gold, pouring through a haze of salt and diesel. Children pressed against the railings to feed gulls; a vendor moved down the aisle selling warm curry puffs wrapped in newsprint. Somewhere, a radio hummed a Tamil love song distorted by the wind.

She closed her eyes for a moment, letting the rhythm of the engines become breath, steady, hypnotic. The sea smelled of rust and clove, faint traces of oil and dried kelp. Beneath the mechanical thrum, she could almost feel the deeper pulse of the channel, the old maritime artery that had once carried Chola traders and Srivijayan monks between worlds. Each swell felt like a page turning under her palms.

Three hours later, Langkawi rose from the haze; emerald cliffs, white beaches, the dense green crown of Gunung Raya cutting into cloud. The ferry docked with a low clang. Heat spilled onto the deck. Selena stepped ashore, her scarf fluttering against her shoulder, the air heavier, sweeter here, thick with frangipani and seaweed.

A woman waved from beyond the customs gate, field-shirt rolled at the sleeves, a flash of intelligence in her eyes.

"Dr Ravenscroft? I'm Noorani Hassan, University Science Malaysia. Welcome to our little furnace."

They shook hands. Noorani's palm was warm, sun-toughened. "We'll take my car, it's about forty minutes inland to the Mahsuri Cultural Reserve. I'll drive slow; the cows don't care about PhDs."

The road unfurled through coconut groves and rice fields gone silver in the heat. Motorbikes buzzed past with baskets of durian and herbs. The car smelled faintly of coffee and sea salt.

"You've heard the legend?" Noorani asked as they climbed toward the foothills.

Selena nodded. "A woman accused of betrayal. Her blood ran white."

"Mahsuri," Noorani said softly. "Cursed the island for seven generations. People used to whisper that every drought, every storm, was her sorrow echoing. Maybe she was more truth than myth; one of those women history couldn't make peace with."

Selena looked out the window. Palm fronds blurred, sunlight breaking on wet leaves. "Seems we keep meeting her kind across time."

"That's why you're here," Noorani replied. "To let the silenced speak."

The road narrowed, climbing into forest. A sudden breeze carried the scent of rain and crushed lime. Through the trees, Selena glimpsed a cluster of tents and scaffolds, white against the red earth.

Noorani slowed the car. "There," she said. "Kota Mahsuri Heritage Zone. The stone's waiting."

At the Dig Site

The air inside the tent was cooler, smelling faintly of clay and rain.

At its centre lay a rectangular pit no deeper than a man's height. Within it, half-embedded in coral sediment, was the stone; smooth, honey-grey, etched with the faint curls of ancient Tamil-Brahmi.

Noorani crouched beside it. "We found this two days ago, half-buried under a collapsed drainage wall. Look here, the inscription curves inward, mirrored from the Penang fragment you mentioned in your paper."

Selena knelt, brushing a wisp of sand from the carved lines. The sunlight caught the grooves, and for a moment, the script seemed to glint like wet bronze.

Her breath slowed. "It's reversed. As if it was meant to face its twin."

Noorani nodded. "Exactly. One speaks fire. The other, breath. Together they form a phrase: *agni vayu*. Fire beneath air. Or..." she smiled faintly, "perhaps your favourite; fire beneath salt."

Selena looked up, pulse quickening. "Then this completes the invocation. The Gate of Breath wasn't a metaphor, it's a code of elements."

"Or a prayer beneath the stone," Noorani said quietly.

Selena let her palm rest against the surface, just a heartbeat. The stone was cool, then warm, as if it exhaled through her skin. A pulse, faint but alive. She didn't flinch, she just breathed with it.

When she drew her hand back, she felt grounded, not dazed. The energy didn't shatter her this time, it settled inside her, like recognition finally accepted.

Langkawi – by the Water, Evening

Her hotel, The Gasing, was less a hotel than a weathered wooden shack on stilts at the water's edge, the sort of place that smelled of salt, coconut husk, and quiet. The sea lapped against the posts beneath her window, a constant whisper in the humid dusk. A single ceiling fan clicked overhead like an old metronome.

After a quick shower and a promise to meet Noorani later for dinner, Selena sat cross-legged by the open window. Outside, the mangroves rustled; a heron dipped through the shallows. Lanterns bobbed faintly along the jetty, casting trembling halos across the tide.

She took a slow breath, exhaling into stillness.

The energy from the stone hadn't left; it pulsed low in her palms and spine, a quiet hum threading through her pulse.

She closed her eyes and whispered Soren's grounding cue:

"Root to earth. Breath to fire. Memory to light."

The hum deepened. The sea breeze pressed gently against her skin, warm as breath. Behind her lids, the red of the sunset turned to ember, then to the molten gold she'd seen inside the script's grooves.

And then came the sound, soft at first, then rising; the rhythm of water meeting shore, until it became a heartbeat not her own.

Salt. Fire. Breath.

The same triad.

The same vow.

When she opened her eyes again, the light had shifted to indigo. The tide was higher. The moon floated low and gold. She wasn't shaken this time, only alert, like a tuning fork struck true.

The island was alive around her.

And for the first time, she could feel it listening back.

....

Dream Trace – Langkawi Shoreline, Circa 11th Century CE

The hum of the sea folded into silence, and then into sound again — not the present tide, but an older one. Selena's breath slowed. The shack dissolved into horizon. The wooden floor beneath her became wet sand.

She stood barefoot on a moonlit shore. The air smelled of rain, lotus, and clove. Far beyond, torches burned along Srivijayan cliffs, their reflections trembling across the tide.

She was no longer Selena. She was **Mayilai**; emissary of Rajendra Chola, scholar of sea codes, flame-bearer of the southern empire.

Wind tangled her veil. The copper bangles at her wrists chimed softly. Behind her, monks in saffron stood in half-circle reverence; ahead, the altar stone waited, carved with twin serpents and the falcon sigil.

She placed her palms upon it. The surface thrummed, cool first, then warm, as though exhaling through her skin. A pulse beneath stone answered her heartbeat.

From the cliffs, a chant rose, Buddhist intonation blending with Tamil syllables, the cadence of two civilisations meeting mid-sea.

Mayilai lifted her face to the waves and whispered:

"Breathe fire into salt, that remembrance may cross the world."

The sea brightened. Foam curled around her ankles. The scroll in her hand began to shimmer, its palm leaves inscribed with the invocation she had guarded since Oman.

She untied the serpent-thread. The words on the scroll burned like light under water.

She didn't read them aloud.

She became them.

Her breath synchronized with the tide. The vibration rose from her chest, through her throat; pure resonance, not language. The scroll dissolved into the sea like golden ash.

The wind softened. A falcon circled once above the cliffs and vanished.

And then the voice — his voice — emerged through mist:

"You've crossed the breath, but not the fire."

She turned, but he was already gone. Only footprints remained, swallowed by the tide.

Mayilai closed her eyes, whispered into the wind:

"Then let the fire remember us both."

The sea glowed once more, then darkened into night.

....

Transition Back – Gasing Beach Hut, Langkawi

Selena opened her eyes. The world returned slowly, like a film reel warming to motion.

The tide outside had risen to kiss the stilts of her room. The candle beside her had nearly burned out.

She wasn't trembling. She was alert, steady; as if every breath now carried an echo older than her body.

The island wasn't giving her visions anymore.

It was giving her back her role.

Outside, the night sea shimmered like molten glass.

Flash Memory – The Professor's Voice

She leaned back against the wall, eyes half closed, and for a fleeting moment she heard it, Suresh's voice, not in the room, but in memory.

Low, warm, deliberate. The kind of voice that could make even silence sound intelligent.

"Lena," he had said once, back in Melbourne, during a quiet evening in the archives.

"You keep chasing proof like it's going to save you. But some knowledge doesn't want to be proven. It wants to be remembered."

She could see him now as clearly as if he stood before her; sleeves rolled up, glasses hanging from his collar, that faint smile when he caught her watching. He always spoke like he was half in this world, half in another.

"You think these fragments; these seals, these scripts — are records," he'd continued.

"They're not. They're mirrors. The more you study them, the more they study you."

At the time, she had laughed, brushing off the mysticism as Suresh's poetic streak. But now, in the thick Langkawi air, his words pulsed through her like veins made of light.

She rose and walked to the small writing desk by the window. The notebook lay open where she'd left it that afternoon. The page still held the rough pencil sketch of the mirrored inscriptions; fire and breath, two elements circling each other like opposites meant to touch but never merge.

She picked up her pencil, hand steady despite the tremor under her skin, and wrote beneath the drawing:

"They're not doors. They're frequencies."

Then, almost without thinking, she turned the pencil sideways and shaded two small falcons above the words; one facing east, one west.

For a long while, she just sat there, listening to the tide.

Somewhere beyond the mangroves, thunder muttered; not a storm yet, just the sound of the island clearing its throat.

She closed her eyes again, and in the quiet between heartbeats, Suresh's voice returned, softer this time, almost fond.

"You're not excavating ruins, Lena. You're excavating yourself. Don't be afraid when the layers look familiar."

A smile flickered at the edge of her lips. "Too late," she whispered into the dark.

Outside, the moon slipped behind a cloud, and the shack seemed to breathe with her; wooden planks creaking in rhythm, the whole structure alive and listening.

The hum she'd felt since Oman; that low vibration at the base of her spine, rose again. But this time, it didn't overwhelm. It aligned.

She exhaled slowly and whispered into the room:

"I hear you."

The fan clicked twice, then stilled. The island held its breath.

Reflections – Langkawi Dusk

By dusk, the world had turned to amber and smoke.

From her window at The Gasing, Selena watched the light drain slowly across the water, softening the edges of the mangroves until they looked half-dreamed. The tide had pulled back, leaving behind a patchwork of reflected sky; streaks of rose, gold, and indigo trembling with every ripple.

Somewhere down the shore, fishermen were calling to each other in Malay, their laughter low and melodic. A child's kite, bright red floated high above the beach, catching the last fire of the sun. The scent of grilled fish with sambal (local seafood grill dressing or paste) and clove drifted through the air, warm and earthy, grounding her back to now.

She had thought the visions might leave her raw, untethered.

Instead, she felt strangely lucid; aware of both the fragility and fullness of her body, like her skin could finally hold what had always been trying to return.

The hum inside her chest had quietened into something almost musical.

She pressed her fingers lightly to her sternum. "Heart," she whispered, "not storm."

The phrase from Oman came back to her; She who seeks fire beneath salt shall find the gate of breath.

Now, it no longer felt like a riddle.

It felt like anatomy.

Fire — the spark that moved through lifetimes.

Salt — the memory that bound them.

Breath — the bridge that made remembering possible.

The Gate of Breath wasn't a monument waiting to be uncovered. It was this, the alignment of pulse, will, and memory. A remembering that required embodiment, not excavation.

She rose, wrapping a shawl loosely around her shoulders, and stepped out onto the narrow jetty. The planks were cool beneath her feet. The tide lapped against the stilts like the slow heartbeat of the island itself.

Out there, beyond the black curve of sea, lay the next point of the map; Guangzhou, the eastern corridor of the maritime routes.

The name flickered in her mind not as destination, but as resonance.

If Langkawi was the bridge, then Guangzhou was the echo.

She exhaled softly, the way Soren had taught her: a surrender, not a sigh.

Behind her, the lights of The Gasing glowed diml; one window, one candle.

Before her, the sea stretched vast and dark, and yet she didn't feel alone.

A single falcon cry cut through the dusk, distant but distinct.

She smiled. Even here, the watcher followed.

She whispered into the salt air, "I'm coming."

The words were neither promise nor defiance, just recognition.

The night folded into silence, fire beneath her ribs, salt on her skin, breath steady in her chest.

Langkawi had remembered her.
Now it was her turn to remember the world.

Selena's Diary Entry

Field Notes – Langkawi / Kota Mahsuri Site

Mission:

Survey inscription stone uncovered near Mahsuri site – parallels to Penang Tamil-Brahmi fragment. Energy resonance detected during physical contact; stone carries serpent-falcon dual motif (11th century Chola–Srivijaya alignment). Dream Trance revealed continuity between the Oman "Gate of Breath" and Langkawi's "Mirror of Salt" invocation.

Integration phase achieved – fire, salt, and breath now recognised as energetic triad linking lifetimes (Vellichi → Mayilai → Selena).

Dream Trace Summary:

Mayilai performs tide ritual — dissolves scroll into sea. The phrase "Breathe fire into salt" repeats. Falcon motif present.

Chakra Thread:

Root & Solar Plexus: Grounding achieved through Langkawi coastline (physical embodiment of lineage memory).

Heart Expansion: Activation during trance upon scroll dissolution — grief transmuted to remembrance.

Crown Bridge: Connection with Dr Suresh's guidance — "They're not doors, they're frequencies."

Selena's Reflection:

Langkawi was not discovery — it was absorption.

The island didn't offer proof, it offered permission.

Mayilai dissolved the scroll into sea foam; I've done the same with fear.

Mahsuri's legend lingers here — woman wronged, purity tested, truth vindicated only after death. Perhaps that's why the island hums like forgiveness.

Suresh was right — these artefacts aren't records. They're mirrors.

And I am finally starting to see what's reflected back.

Keywords:

- Langkawi–Srivijaya link
- Fire–Salt–Breath continuum
- Mahsuri resonance / feminine vindication
- Mayilai trance reactivation
- Kota Mahsuri stone (serpent–falcon dual seal)
- Guangzhou alignment – "Echo Port" next threshold
- The watcher still follows — falcon above dusk line

Chapter Nine – The City of Soundless Names

Transition — From Langkawi to Penang

The ferry to Penang cut through pale dawn waters, the horizon lifting in slow amber folds. Selena sat on the upper deck, hair loose, salt threading her skin. The island behind her glowed like memory; warm, reluctant to let go.

She watched as Langkawi shrank into mist, a scatter of green peaks over a restless sea.

The ferry hummed beneath her, a deep, living sound. Around her, families slept, tourists scrolled through phones, but Selena only watched the water, mesmerised by the way the tide seemed to breathe with her.

By the time the ferry docked at Swettenham Pier, Penang's skyline gleamed under a thin veil of late morning haze. She made her way through the colonial wharf and into the bustle of George Town, the scent of fried shallots and sea air tangling in her wake. Her hotel from earlier in the week still held her booking; she spent one quiet night repacking, reviewing her notes, and emailing Samira and Dr Suresh.

By dawn, she was at the airport, passport in hand, bound for Guangzhou.

Guangzhou – Arrival, Present Day

The morning flight from Penang to Kuala Lumpur was short, just under an hour, but it felt like crossing a threshold.

As the plane lifted over the Straits, the island fell away beneath her; green hills fading into mist, fishing boats trailing silver wakes through the water. She pressed her palm to the window, as if to hold on a little longer. Penang had been warmth, rhythm, recognition. But Guangzhou — Guangzhou was calling with a different frequency.

At Kuala Lumpur International, the transit terminal buzzed with the scent of roasted coffee and sandalwood perfume, the sound of rolling suitcases, and soft announcements echoing across glass walls. Selena found a quiet corner near her gate and ordered tea which she didn't touch. Her reflection shimmered faintly in the window, half-shadowed by the bright runway outside.

Emotionally, she felt split between clarity and ache.

Her mind wanted data; trade routes, inscriptions, confirmed timelines.

Her heart wanted meaning; why the visions came, why the sea kept calling her by name.

Spiritually, she hovered between surrender and control. Meditation had steadied her in Langkawi, but now she could feel something new stirring beneath the calm; a pull not of curiosity, but destiny.

She pulled her scarf tighter, grounding herself in its faint scent of clove and sea salt. The same scarf she'd worn since Muscat. It felt like armour now, or a map she hadn't yet learned to read.

When her boarding call echoed, she closed her eyes for a moment and inhaled; slow, deliberate, centering.

I'm ready, she thought.

Not to find proof, but to find remembrance.

On the flight to Guangzhou, she didn't read or watch films. She simply sat with her breath, syncing it to the low hum of the engines. Each inhale felt like collecting fragments of her past lives; each exhale, a quiet release of what no longer served her.

By the time the aircraft began its descent, clouds bruised with dusk parted to reveal a river of light, below, the Pearl River twisting through the heart of the city like a silver brushstroke. The city unfurled around her like an ancient scroll, high-rise reflections cast across the Pearl River, stone bridges lit in soft gold, and hidden within it all, the ghosts of maritime centuries.

Selena pressed her forehead lightly against the plane window, watching as a city of glass and stone bloomed from the river's edge like a modern calligraphy stroke, fluid and unending.

Guangzhou didn't welcome her.

It appraised her.

Selena smiled faintly at the thought. Maybe that's what I've become too, a vessel for buried histories trying to breathe again.

Guangzhou shimmered with contradiction. Ancient alleyways wove between tech towers. Street hawkers flanked Gucci billboards. At first glance, it was a city of commerce. But beneath the neon and steel, history pulsed like a buried river.

Selena stepped off the plane and into Baiyun International's arrivals hall, a subtle discomfort set in. Not fear, just dissonance. Mandarin echoed all around her, fast and musical, impossible to decipher. Signs blinked in characters she couldn't read. Even at the taxi stand, English dissolved into gestures and numbered printouts.

And yet, the stillness in her chest deepened, not with anxiety, but recognition. This silence was familiar. Not from this life, but another.

Her hotel sat near Shamian Island, where the Pearl River curved like a painted dragon through the city. The room overlooked colonial façades, balconies with carved balustrades, banyan trees lean into cobbled streets, their roots climbing old colonial walls. Across the street, elderly men played xiangqi under flickering lanterns. Steam from noodle carts twisted upward like incense.

This city feels like an archive, she thought. But everything's redacted.

She dropped her bags. Didn't unpack. Just opened the window and breathed.

Ink and incense, she thought.

Mango peel and engine fumes. And rain. Always rain.

The disorientation was sharp, but not unpleasant. She hadn't come to be comfortable. She had come to listen.

That night, sleep hovered at the edge of her mind but didn't land. Her dreams tangled with faint chimes and ink-stained scrolls. Her dreams were stitched with half-translated syllables. Bells that didn't ring. Names that wouldn't hold still.

Maritime Silk Road Museum — Present Day

In the morning, she didn't arranged a personal guide. Not here. In Oman, she'd had Farid. In Penang, there was Meera. But here, something told her she needed anonymity, distance from the story she was inside. So she joined a quiet local history walking tour, blending into a small group of scholars and curious travelers.

They began at the Whampoa Anchorage, once a Chola port of call, and walked north to Canton's Thirteen Factories, then toward a weathered temple tucked behind an herbal medicine hall.

Their tour guide, Lina, welcomed them in accented English at the entrance to the Maritime Silk Road Museum.

"Today we walk through memory," Lina said. "But not the kind in books. The kind buried in stone and trade."

The exhibit hall stretched cool and dim before them, silk banners fluttering faintly from the ceiling, their faded gold threads catching the light.

Selena drifted behind the others, lingering before a glass display of bilingual stone inscriptions, Tamil and Chinese, etched side by side.

"This tablet," Lina announced, "was recovered from the Song court records. A record of foreign merchant guilds granted royal protection. Tamil script here notes the name of the guild, Ainnurruvar."

Selena's chest pulled tight. The same guild she'd seen referenced in Zanzibar.

But something else caught her eye.

A smaller stone, behind the main display. Its Tamil was partially worn, but the Chinese was sharp.

And one phrase leapt at her.

"女聲無名"

The woman with soundless names.

Her breath stilled. It wasn't just the phrase, it was the echo. Like it had been waiting for her.

Lina turned. "You may explore this floor for fifteen minutes before we move upstairs."

The others drifted on.

Selena found a bench beneath an illustrated ceiling scroll and sat, palms on her knees, breath slow.

She didn't close her eyes.

She didn't need to.

Her gaze flickered from the inscriptions to the silk banners. Her body relaxed, not with exhaustion, but surrender.

And softly, almost imperceptibly, she whispered inwardly: "Guide me, if I'm ready."

The space above her scalp warmed. A familiar sensation, as if a quiet breath passed through the top of her skull. She'd felt it before. With Soren, during meditation. That first time, he'd named it: crown chakra awakening, the opening of the thousand-petaled lotus, the bridge between self and soul.

But she didn't need names now.

She only needed permission.

And then, the room shifted.

The world dimmed.

Not into blackness, but into brush-stroke light, like an ink wash painting unraveling itself.

....

Dream Trace — The Court of Silence, Song Dynasty, Circa 11th Century CE

She stood in a lacquered corridor lined with silk scrolls and brass lanterns. She, was Mayilai, not Vellichi, wore robes of deep bronze and amethyst, her hair twisted high, studded with crushed pearls.

This wasn't the shoreline of Zanzibar.

This was the court of the Song Dynasty, and she was not a servant. Not a merchant.

She was something rarer.

A Tamil emissary-scholar, invited by the royal court to exchange knowledge between empires. Her presence here was earned, not by title, but by the scrolls she carried.

Whispers followed her footsteps.

"The woman of no name."

"The foreign oracle."

"The one who writes sound with silence."

She was led into a chamber of stone and sandalwood, where a figure waited beneath gauze drapery.

A woman. Barely older than Mayilai.

Clad in silvery robes stitched with phoenixes. Her face was luminous, poised, the bearing of royalty, but with eyes that shimmered with curiosity.

"I have read your poem," the woman said in Mandarin.

And somehow, Mayilai responded. In perfect Mandarin.

"It was not written. It was felt."

The woman smiled faintly. "You feel in a language we do not yet have words for."

"Perhaps the soul is a script older than speech," Mayilai offered.

The princess drew closer.

"They call me Princess Gongshu." She lowered her voice. "But between us, names are irrelevant."

"你不属于这里。但我认识你。"

You do not belong here. But I know you.

And Mayilai, without pause, continued in flawless Mandarin.

"姊妹之间，不需归属。"

Between sisters, there is no need to belong.

Selena, watching from within the vision, felt her own mind bend, recognising words she should not know. Language unfurled in her memory like it had lived there always.

The princess pressed a silk square into Mayilai's palm. On it: six silent bells embroidered in gold thread, with Tamil-Brahmi beneath:

நாமமில்லா பத்து

The Ten Without Names.

"Return when the silence breaks," the princess whispered.

Then, the court faded like mist.

....

Reflections — Shamian Courtyard, Evening

Selena blinked back into the room, breath shallow, fingers curled against her thighs.

The tour group was already drifting toward the next exhibit. She rose slowly, heart still thudding in a rhythm not quite her own, and followed. She nodded absently at Lina's commentary on Tang-era porcelain and Song maritime maps, her mind a blur of Mandarin syllables and silk robes.

After the group dispersed into the final wing, Selena slipped outside to the museum's courtyard garden, a serene pocket of bamboo, sun-warmed stone, and quietly trickling water. She ordered jasmine tea from the café kiosk and let the steam warm her fingers. The sunlight, filtered through tall banana leaves, spilled gold across her lap.

Only then did she allow herself to breathe deeply. The ache in her chest remained, not pain, but a pressure to understand. To remember.

She opened her tablet and sent an email to Dr. Suresh.

Subject: Urgent – Song Dynasty Tamil-Chinese Connections

Dr. Suresh,

While in my museum tour in Guangzhou, I see Chola stone tablets with Tamil language being exchanges with the Song Dynasty. I was also informed by the tour guide that the Chola ambassadors were able to speak and maybe read and written Mandarin. This was established during political, religious and trade route. Could there be any record of Tamil emissaries speaking Chinese this early? Any cultural or religious links that might explain this?

—Selena

The reply came later that evening.

From: Dr. Suresh

Subject: Re: Song Dynasty & Tamil Links

Selena,

What you're describing would be unrecorded, but not impossible. Tamil merchant guilds (Ainnurruvar, Manigramam) were known to operate in Song China. Court alliances likely occurred. But no verified accounts of Tamil emissaries fluent in Mandarin exist.

Still... it's worth investigating.

Contact: **Professor Zhao Lin** – Institute for Studies of the Maritime Silk Road, Sun Yat-sen University

I've cc'd her. She's cautious, but curious.

—Suresh

Selena closed the laptop slowly. The chimes above the courtyard door stirred. But made no sound.

And yet, the silence felt like it had just spoken.

She exhaled slowly,
as if remembering something her body had always known.

Selena's Diary Entry

Field Notes — Guangzhou / Yuexiu Pavilion

Mission:

Investigate Ainnurruvar trade influence and Tamil inscriptions in Song China

Phrase Repeated (Trance):

"你不属于这里。但我认识你。"" (*You do not belong here. But I know you.*)

"Return when the silence breaks."

Artifact Seen:

Silk square with six embroidered bells; phrase in Tamil-Brahmi: *The Ten Without Names*

Chakra Thread:

Crown & Throat: Activation through linguistic memory — language as vibration, not translation.

Heart: Expansion via sisterhood recognition — Princess Gongshu as mirror soul archetype.

Selena's Reflection:

I heard Mandarin in my own voice. I felt her memories as if they were braided into mine.

She wasn't a diplomat. She was a bridge.

Not between kingdoms—but between languages, symbols, and silence.

Keywords:

- Tamil–Song Dynasty merchant guilds
- Soundless names / sacred silence
- Soul memory of language
- Sisterhood across empires
- Veiled archives in court halls

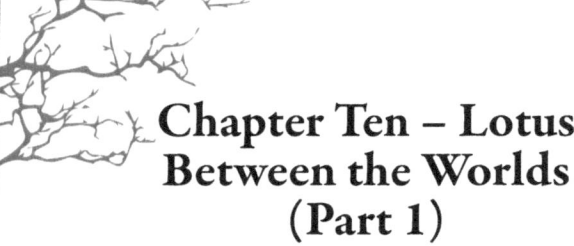

Chapter Ten – Lotus Between the Worlds (Part 1)

Guangzhou — Morning Rain – Present Day

The rain in Guangzhou wasn't unkind.

It didn't slash or sweep. It softened a cool, misted hush that cloaked the Pearl River like breath against a mirror.

Selena stepped from the metro onto the tree-lined boulevard that ran along the eastern wall of Sun Yat-sen University. Her scarf, still damp from the morning drizzle, clung gently to her collarbone. This wasn't like Penang's salty monsoon heat or Oman's bone-dry winds. This was subtler. Thick with magnolia and incense, the scent of old books and colder dynasties.

She was here to meet Professor Zhao Lin, a literary historian whom Dr. Suresh had recommended after failing to locate Tamil sources in the Guangzhou archives.

"She has a reputation," Suresh had said. "Quiet genius. Old school. If there's a thread between China and Tamil Nadu that hasn't been pulled, he'll know."

The Meeting — Institute for Studies of the Maritime Silk Road

Selena arrived at Sun Yat-sen University, navigating through a quiet courtyard framed by rain-polished stone and the scent of camphor trees. The campus was dignified, understated, a world apart from the commercial clang of the city's outer districts.

Professor Zhao Lin greeted her beneath the awning of the Institute for Studies of the Maritime Silk Road, her umbrella tilted sideways in greeting. Mid-fifties, eyes sharp behind rounded glasses, she wore a pressed cream tunic over navy slacks, and carried a linen folder bound with copper thread.

"You're following ghosts most people forget to remember," she said without preamble. "Tamil inscriptions in China. Female emissaries. Pearls passed like coded treaties. You've come chasing Tamil echoes and they do exist."

Selena smiled, surprised and relieved. "Then I'm not mad?"

"Oh, you probably are," Zhao Lin said dryly. "But only the useful kind. Come, I'll show you something."

The Archive Chamber — Discovery and Recognition

In the quiet of Zhao Lin's office, lined wall-to-wall with manuscripts and tea canisters, she unrolled a protective scroll tube and produced a Tamil-Chinese bilingual verse, a rare archival reproduction from the Quanzhou Maritime Museum.

"This was found a decade ago, near a temple complex further east," Zhao Lin said. "The Tamil is poetic. Your people brought verse with their trade. But this... the Chinese half is strange. Not quite Confucian. Not Buddhist either."

Selena leaned closer. She didn't translate. She absorbed.

The Tamil lines were familiar in tone, she could feel the rhythm:

"From lotus-bloom to mountain root,
The map is not drawn in ink, but vow."

She blinked. That line, vow. Her breath caught.

"Does this connect with a princess of the Song court?" she asked. "Xu Lian?"

Zhao Lin's brow lifted. "She is mentioned only in minor footnotes. Why do you ask?"

Selena explained, carefully, not the visions, but the memory of encountering the name in her research. A diplomatic woman, a keeper of private salons. A whisper in the archive.

Zhao Lin poured chrysanthemum tea into two porcelain cups. "You speak of Xu Lian like she was a reflection. Many think her lineage was inspired by another woman, older, greater. Wu Zhao, Empress Wu Zetian."

"Wu Zetian," Selena repeated. "Wasn't she a concubine-turned-empress?"

"Indeed. The only woman to rule as emperor in her own name. A master of language. A weaver of political truth through poetry, scroll, and silence. Xu Lian studied her surviving fragments in secret. She founded a circle of women and eunuchs, scribes who communicated in symbol, not speech. Few records survive. But it was said they could rewrite the court's mood with a single line."

She paused, studying her face.

"Does this interest you for academic reasons? Or is it something else?"

Selena didn't answer. Not with words. Her fingers gently traced the lotus emblem printed at the scroll's edge.

Something pulled at her; not her mind, but somewhere behind her brow, like a curtain lifting.

Third Eye...the guide within. See what already knows you.

She nodded once. "Mainly academic purpose...but it's both," she said. "I think I knew her. Or someone like her."

Professor Zhao Lin stood and smoothed the edge of her linen tunic. "There's something I'd like to show you before we continue," she said, voice low but certain.

Silk Road Maritime Heritage Wing — The Mirror and the Fire

They walked through the marble-floored corridor of the university's humanities wing. Tall lattice windows cast soft light across carved wooden panels. They passed an archival mural of Chinese junks at sea and arrived at a side entrance marked:

Silk Road Maritime Heritage – Special Collections (English & Multilingual)

The air was cooler here. Still. Laced with the scent of old paper and preserved silk.

Zhao Lin walked Selena past a glass cabinet holding a Song Dynasty mirror engraved with cranes and lotus petals.

"This," she said, "belonged to a noblewoman of the Song court, believed to be Princess Gongshu. Some texts refer to her as 'Xu Lian,' a name scholars suspect she adopted in sacred texts or secret writings, especially those tied to Daoist ritual or Buddhist metaphysics. There's a theory that she belonged to a knowledge circle aligned with spiritual emissaries from the south."

Selena blinked. "From the Chola Empire?"

Professor Zhao nodded slowly. "It's more than possible. These alliances were rarely formal, but they ran deep, especially through women. Xu Lian was known for her skill in poetic symbolism and sacred geometry. Her correspondences where hidden in metaphoric glyphs and silk embroidery, show astonishing parallels to Tamil ritual codes. It's why some believe the Chola emissaries didn't just bring trade, but tantra."

Selena felt the breath catch in her lungs.

"In her scrolls," she continued, "Xu Lian refers to another woman, veiled, foreign, whom she called The Fire-Bearer. That term, incidentally, appears in a Chola temple record we've only recently deciphered."

Something inside Selena flickered. That phrase again. Fire.

"I think," Zhao Lin said gently, "you may want to read this alone. You'll find what you need in the final case near the window, English-translation of Song court poetry and Silk Road feminine correspondences. If anything finds you... come to my office. Or I'll find you later."

She turned with a respectful nod and left her in the stillness of the archive.

Selena crossed the room slowly. A silk banner fluttered from the overhead vent, six lotus petals, veined with gold.

She reached the final reading desk, trailed her fingers along the edges of a worn anthology, and sat. Outside, rain gently threaded the windowpane.

....

Dream Trace — The Fire-Court Scroll, Song Dynasty, Circa 11th Century CE

The rain whispered against the glass.

Selena approached the final case, trailing her fingers across its wooden edge.

The banner above her fluttered faintly, six lotus petals veined in gold.

She opened a bilingual anthology. Tamil and Mandarin verses wove like twin flames.

Each page she turned hummed, not read, but remembered.

Her pulse began to rise. She wasn't choosing the texts. They were choosing her.

One line stopped her breath:

"The emissary from the fire-court, whose tongue bore two waters; the sea, and the silence."

As she whispered the words, the air around her thickened. The light bent, soft and golden, like sunlight through silk. And there, in that shimmer, a second presence unfolded.

Not seen, but unmistakably felt.

A woman's silhouette, poised yet fluid, robed in imperial red.

The scent of sandalwood and ink drifted through the room. Selena didn't need a name.

The title rose unbidden in her mind, ancient and precise: Wu Zetian.

The empress's voice was neither loud nor human. It moved through Selena's chest like breath caught between two centuries.

"The Fire-Bearer returns when silence forgets its name."

The phrase struck like recognition. Not vision. Not imagination. A message.

Selena blinked hard, the image fading, but the vibration remained; a pulse behind her brow, her third eye warming as if a seal had opened.

She wrote the phrase down, hand trembling.

The emissary from the fire-court, whose tongue bore two waters; the sea, and the silence.

This was not history. It was inheritance.

Time lost its edges. Hours passed unnoticed, until Zhao Lin's voice gently brought her back.

"You've been here all day," she said. "Did you find what you were looking for?"

"I... don't know yet," Selena admitted. "But I found things that felt like they were looking for me."

"Then you're in the right place."

....

Reflections — The Pearl River Café, Evening

That evening, over hand-pulled noodles and lotus tea at a quiet café tucked beside the Pearl River embankment, the two women sat across from each other, as scholar and seeker.

They didn't talk of visions. Only of patterns.

Zhao Lin tapped her chopsticks gently. "There are poems in our archives that scholars have dismissed for decades because the metaphors don't make sense in pure Chinese context. But... if you read them with Dravidian spiritual metaphors, suddenly it all aligns.

The spirals. The veiled fire. The mirrors.

Selena nodded, slowly. "I found a scroll with layered symbology today, lotus patterns, twin flames, seal phrases that echoed the falcon motif from Dhofar."

Zhao's eyes sparkled. "There were Chola envoys in the Song court. That's confirmed by the Song Huiyao Jigao. The Ainnurruvar guild had merchant rights in Guangzhou. But this", she leaned closer, "this is not about trade. It's about transmission. Spiritual codes embedded in diplomacy."

Selena said nothing. But inside her, the puzzle was tilting. Something enormous had shifted. The research no longer felt academic. It felt... alive.

Selena returned to her hotel that night with a backpack of photocopied notes, a voice recorder full of murmured observations, and a new resolve.

The research had spoken.

But the answers, the dangerous ones would come tomorrow.

Some books held answers. Others held mirrors.
But tonight, she had opened a door,
and whatever waited on the other side already knew her name.

Selena's Diary Entry

Field Notes – Guangzhou / Sun Yat-sen University / Museum of Maritime Silk Road Civilisations

Mission:

Meeting with Prof. Zhao Lin to investigate Tamil-Chinese links via Song Dynasty inscriptions.

Accessed the Maritime Silk Road archives, Song court scrolls, bilingual manuscripts, and symbolic correspondences.

Strong intuitive response to Princess Xu Lian and Empress Wu Zetian references.

Phrase Repeated:

"The emissary from the fire-court, whose tongue bore two waters... the sea, and the silence."

Chakra Thread:

Third Eye: Activation through recognition and ancestral memory.

Crown: Expansion through Wu Zetian's archetype — knowledge as illumination.

Selena's Reflection:

This wasn't just research, it was recognition.

I wasn't pulling threads. The threads were pulling me.

The scrolls weren't just stories. They felt like tasks I had once promised to complete.

Professor Zhao Lin spoke of Empress Wu Zetian not as a ruler, but as a signal — a reminder of what happens when feminine power uses silence instead of steel.

Xu Lian may have been her student in spirit.

And Mayilai, in that life, was something more: a transmitter between empires. Not to bring war. But truth.

The codes were in the pearls. In the poetry.

In me.

And when I sat in that archive, I didn't blink into a vision.

I stepped into a knowing.

This is not just memory.

This is calling.

Purpose:

And I feel it now, not as memory, but as momentum.

Keywords:

- Chola–Song diplomacy
- Past life linguistic memory
- Third eye activation
- Sacred skills / court scribes
- Xu Lian (possible soul sister / guide)
- Crown chakra opening through conscious breath
- Memory not as history but as continuity

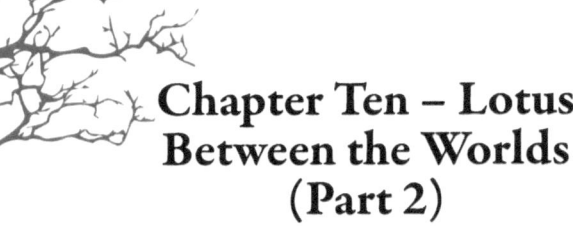

Chapter Ten – Lotus
Between the Worlds
(Part 2)

Guangzhou, China — Before Sunrise – Present Day
Selena's second morning at Sun Yat-sen University
began before sunrise. She skipped the hotel breakfast and
arrived at the library just as the custodians unlocked the carved
bronze doors. The reading room welcomed her like it
remembered her, the lotus-etched window still fogged with
early rain.

She opened her notebook and began a grid.

Century	Region	Identity	Scroll/Seal Clue
2nd CE	South India / Oman	Velliche	Twin serpents, salt rites
11th CE	Zanzibar, Persia	Mayilai	Falcon seal, diplomatic oath
Present	Global	Selena	Cross-referenced fragments

At first, the pattern was instinctual. Then it became
irrefutable.

"I wasn't just dreaming their lives. I was continuing them."

She opened A Maritime History of the Chola Empire, a
weighty English-Chinese volume archived in the global trade

corridor section. The deeper she read, the clearer the map became.

The library's microfilm records revealed Tamil inscriptions from the Ainnurruvar guild, merchant-priests, diplomats, and financiers were stationed in Song China ports under imperial protection.

Selena highlighted every passage, then transferred it all to a digital timeline.

"The sea wasn't a border for the Cholas," she whispered to herself. "It was a bloodstream."

Selena's Journal – Day One

Discovery:

Velliche and Mayilai lived centuries apart — and yet both appear during phases of naval expansion. What if I'm remembering these lives now because something in the *route* remembers me?

Feeling:

Third eye tingles. Like someone is standing behind my thoughts — pointing.

Phrase from research:

"Those who carry the fire do not sail alone."

Appears in Tamil–Mandarin inscription from Quanzhou port, 11th century.

Historical Notes — Chola Maritime Campaigns

The Great Naval Campaign of Rajendra Chola I

- 1025 CE: Rajendra Chola I launches a massive naval expedition across the Bay of Bengal, defeating the Srivijaya Empire and establishing Tamil presence in Sumatra, the Malay Peninsula, and the western ports of China.

● Alliances were struck not only through conquest, but through diplomatic placement of Tamil generals, who intermarried with local royalty.

● The Cholas controlled maritime trade routes across Southeast Asia through naval mastery and sacred emissaries, not just merchants.

Chola inscriptions were found in Quanzhou, Kedah, Takuapa, and Nagapattinam, indicating a network far broader than previously believed.

Day Two: Knowledge Codes and Karmic Links

At lunch, Zhao Lin joined her with two annotated scroll scans.

"There's something curious about this Song court letter," Zhao said, tapping a poetic line. "This mentions a woman emissary from the Southern Sea who spoke in mirror logic. The term appears again and again."

Selena studied the phrase.

Mirror logic: language spoken between truths.

Zhao explained: "Princess Gongshu had a known spiritual advisor named Xu Lian, half-Tamil, half-Cantonese. There's a court poem describing her as 'a lotus risen through two waters.' She likely trained with temple scribes from a Southern dynasty."

Selena paused over her notes, her pen resting against the page.

It struck her how empires never really invented power, they inherited it, refined it, renamed it. The Cholas had known this long before the British ever drew their maps. Raja Raja Chola had built not just ships but a philosophy of the sea; one that treated water as a living artery of commerce, diplomacy, and divine rhythm. His fleets sailed beyond sight, not to conquer but to connect, carrying stone inscriptions, temple fire, and trade in equal measure.

Centuries later, the British would claim their own mastery of the oceans, formalising a "two-power standard," ensuring their navy was larger than the next two combined. But to Selena, that sounded less like innovation and more like memory; the echo of an older empire that had once ruled these waters with copper seals and sacred vows.

Power, she realised, was not born in the Atlantic. It had first breathed in the Bay of Bengal.

She had seen her.

That was the woman from her vision. The princess. But now the name Xu Lian anchored the memory.

"She wasn't just royalty," Selena whispered. "She was a link."

Selena's Email to Dr. Suresh (sent 5:54 p.m.)

Subject: Urgent: Chola–Song Scribe Crossovers

Dear Dr. Suresh,

I've cross-referenced Tamil-Chinese inscriptions in Quanzhou and Guangzhou. Multiple sources confirm Chola presence. But here's the stunning part, poetic exchanges, philosophical dialogues, even spiritual training between Tamil emissaries and Chinese female scribes.

Could Mayilai have been trained as a code-speaker? A soul emissary, not just a diplomat?

Please advise if Tiruvasagam scrolls mention veiled pacts. I'll stay in Guangzhou one more week. This thread feels alive.

Warmly,

Selena

Selena's Journal – Day Two
Discovery:
Xu Lian and Mayilai may have belonged to a shared lineage,not by blood, but by soul contract. Their dialogue was spiritual diplomacy, encoded through scrolls and gestures.
Feeling:
Deja vu growing stronger. When I hold certain pages, my palms heat. Is this what remembering through the third eye feels like?
Phrase:
"Two waters, one fire."
Day Three: Soul Contract and Future Path
Zhao Lin met Selena near the river for tea. The sunset burned gold through the smog.

"You've been quiet today," Zhao observed.

"I'm realising," Selena said slowly, "that this isn't research anymore. It's recognition. Velliche. Mayilai. I lived both."

Zhao didn't flinch. "That's why you're able to see patterns most scholars can't."

Selena unrolled a copy of her timeline map. "The falcon seal, the twin spirals, the mirror logic... All of it isn't just political history. It's karmic. These alliances were soul contracts written long before we had names."

Zhao Lin looked thoughtful. "Maybe you're here not just to decode, but to reactivate."

That night, Selena returned to her hotel room and stood before the mirror. Her reflection looked older somehow, not in face, but in gaze.

"I'm not just a witness," she whispered.

"I'm the continuation."

Flash Memory — The Sea Between Lives

As she turned away from the mirror, a ripple crossed her vision;

Velliche on a Chola deck, salt wind on her face;

Mayilai in the Song court, scrolls in her hands;

and Selena, here, eyes bright with knowing.

Three reflections, one current.

The same flame passing through different time.

She had followed history into silence,
and now silence was speaking back.

Selena's Diary Entry

Field Notes – Sun Yat-sen University, Guangzhou (Library Research Days 1–3)

Mission:

Trace Tamil–Song diplomatic and spiritual intersections. Discover the truth behind Mayilai, Velliche, and my own soul's continuity. Uncover links between sacred emissaries, coded alliances, and karmic maritime expansion.

Chakra Thread:

Third Eye Activation — intuitive access to archetypes and past-life knowledge

Sacral + Solar Plexus Residue — soul contract ignition, embodied purpose

Keywords:

- Mirror logic / encoded spiritual diplomacy
- Chola maritime reach (Quanzhou, Kedah, Takuapa)
- Emissary-scribe alliances
- Rajendra Chola I naval expansion legacy
- Xu Lian / Princess Gongshu connection
- Past-life knowledge as present-life guidance
- Soul contract remembrance
- "Two waters, one fire"

Chapter Eleven –
Letters to the Tiber

Rome, Italy – Present Day

The train hissed as it slid into Termini, the glass of the doors fogging from the weight of a Roman summer. The air inside the cabin was thick with warmth and the faint scent of worn leather and metal rails. Selena stepped out, her breath steady, her steps rehearsed. The marble of the platform radiated midday heat through the soles of her shoes.

She had come to Rome under the guise of a curatorial residency; a collaboration between her institute and the Museo Nazionale Romano, focused on Mediterranean trade networks. But she knew that wasn't the real reason she had accepted. Something had been pulling her west for months, a magnetic, almost cellular pull she could no longer rationalise away.

Her flight had landed in Milan the night before. She had taken the train south that morning, refusing the direct flight to Rome, preferring instead the slow unfolding of landscape: vines crawling over terracotta walls, distant hilltop fortresses, the occasional bell tower breaking the silence like a memory surfacing. Besides a train ride a more romantic than a commercial flight trip.

Now, the city wrapped around her with practiced indifference. Rome didn't seduce, it remembered and awaiting to be discovered.

She slipped into a waiting taxi. The driver didn't ask further questions other than her destination. They wove through tangled arteries of traffic, windows down, the hot wind curling in like incense. The scent of sun-baked stone and diesel, vut occasionally by the shary tang of espresso from the roadside cafes. Selena leaned into the blur, ruins collapsed beside modern scaffolds, ancient domes crouched between banks and pharmacies.

She walked Rome like she'd been here before; not as a tourist, but as someone returning to a room whose furniture had shifted slightly. Past fountains that sang in Latin and ruins that refused to crumble, she arrived at Hotel Forum, her home for the next several days.

The building stood like a hush in the noise, half hidden, wholly aware. Its façade wore time like a cloak: medieval brick wrapped around fragments of forgotten marble, arches that remembered gods, floors that dipped with the weight of centuries. The lobby smelled faintly of lavender and dust.

Her room was simple, elegant. The shutters opened wide to the Forum of Augustus itself, where sunlight fell like gold dust across a broken republic. Temples clawed at the sky with what remained of their ambition.

She set her bag down and let her fingers rest on the stone sill. Then, with quiet ceremony, she popped open a small bottle of champagne, a ritual she saved for cities heavy with ghosts. The cork barely made a sound. She took a slow sip, letting the cold sharpness cut through the heat, letting it anchor her.

The view wasn't just history.

It was geometry.

Memory, cast in shadow and sunlight.

Below her, the broken colonnades of the Forum reached skyward like the ribs of something once divine.

Palazzo Altemps – Late Morning

The air inside the museum was cool and still, touched with the dry scent of stone, aged plaster, and old wood. Somewhere beneath it lingered a quieter note, like forgotten incense absorbed into the walls. Footsteps echoed softly against the marble and tile underfoot as Selena stepped into the vaulted entryway of Palazzo Altemps, the most intimate of the Museo Nazionale Romano's four wings.

Light filtered through high windows, softened by centuries of stone. The building itself breathed with restraint. This wasn't a place that announced its power. It waited for you to listen.

A voice greeted her from behind a pillar.

"Dr Ferini?"

She turned. A man emerged from the side corridor with a leather satchel slung over one shoulder and a pair of nitrile gloves already in his hands. His coat was linen, ivory with a faint crease at the elbow, sleeves rolled carefully above the wrist. Tall, sharp-jawed, with hair that had silvered just enough at the temples to suggest he had once cared deeply about his youth and now no longer needed to.

Dr Matteo Ferini, visiting senior fellow from Sapienza University, gave her a quick, dry smile.

"We weren't sure you'd arrive this morning. Rome in summer has a way of slowing people down."

"I prefer to walk in early, though its almost mid-day" Selena replied. "The light's better. And the noise is less... modern."

"Then you'll enjoy what we've set aside for you."

He led her through a short corridor, speaking as they walked.

"We're digitising a cache from Ostia Antica; mostly export manifest fragments and merchant tokens; but one piece stood out. We thought of your project immediately. It's been languishing in our off-record collections, likely due to its hybrid script."

They passed mosaics faded by time, busts of forgotten emperors, and reliefs of goddesses whose names had outlived their altars. The silence in the corridor felt like pages being turned.

They reached a side room, dimly lit and walled with metal shelving. Inside, a single table had been prepared under a directed light. On it, resting on a neutral grey cloth, sat a blackened slab, its edges worn as if by water or fire.

Dr Matteo stood to one side. Selena pulled on her own gloves.

The stone was roughly the length of her forearm, pitted and uneven. But the inscription was clean, etched with the kind of precision that came from reverence, not routine.

He gestured towards it.

'From the pepper port, by vow, to the keeper of the flame.' That's our translation, at least. The original is a combination of Latin and Tamil-Brahmi, likely inscribed in the first or second century CE. It was recovered near the southern granaries of Ostia, close to what used to be the spice warehouses."

He paused, adjusting the light slightly.

"We believe it came from Muziris, or one of the Tamil ports on the Malabar coast. Black pepper was often traded in sealed packets. This inscription, however, isn't a cargo mark. It's more personal. Some scholars think it's a vow, perhaps even a funerary dedication. I think it's a signal. A coded message embedded in a trade item."

Selena leaned closer, eyes tracing the inscription's curvature.

"A vow... to the keeper of the flame."

"Yes," he said quietly. "Sounds more religious than economic, doesn't it?"

Her fingers, encased in gloves, hovered just above the stone. The grooves shimmered faintly under the light, catching dust motes like secrets rising.

A shiver passed through her, not from cold, but from some internal hinge shifting open.

Vellichi. Cloaked. Waiting. A Roman villa. The weight of a scroll sewn into silk.

The image arrived like breath on glass. Clear, then gone.

Selena straightened, blinking. Her heart thudded once, deep in her chest.

Her eyes caught on something half-hidden beside a tray of amphora shards; a small object, no label.

She reached for it carefully.

An onyx seal. Polished to a dark shine. Warm in her hand, though the room was cool. Its base bore a single word in etched Tamil: மெய் .

— Truth.

She hadn't meant to pick it up. But it was already in her palm. Heavy with memory.

Dr Matteo was still speaking, oblivious.

"There's more in storage, of course. But this piece... I thought you'd recognise it for what it might be. Most don't."

Selena's voice came slow, as if surfacing.

"I think I do."

Selena had spent most of the day moving between the archive lab and the small reading room adjacent to the frescoed galleries. The work had been rewarding, dense layers of old trade documentation, glosses scribbled in marginal Tamil, and inventories from early excavation reports. There were more leads than she'd expected. The stone inscription from Ostia wasn't alone.

The library air was cool and slightly brittle, holding the scent of aged vellum, dust-filtered sunlight, and the soft musk of polished wood. Voices, if they spoke at all, stayed close to a whisper. She had found comfort in that rhythm; search, note, cross-reference, pause but by late afternoon, the weight of the last several weeks caught up with her.

The international flights. The train from Milan. The layers of memory beginning to surface.

She closed her notebook gently and stretched her fingers, flexing out the tightness. Her body felt heavy in the chair.

Dr Matteo passed by with a soft step, a stack of catalogued prints under one arm. His gloves were off now, tucked neatly into his coat pocket.

"Still at it?" he asked, pausing beside her.

Selena gave a tired smile. "I am. But I think it's time to rest the bones."

He nodded in approval. "Wise. It's easy to lose hours in here. The building has that effect."

She slipped her notes into her satchel. "I'll head back to the hotel. I need a proper reset."

"Well," he said, glancing briefly out the window where the sunlight had softened, "if you're up for it later, join me for dinner. The rooftop bar at your hotel has one of the best views in the city. I make a point of going whenever I have a reason."

Selena tilted her head slightly. "That sounds like a good idea."

"Excellent." He smiled and stepped away, already halfway into another corridor before turning back. "Just ask for the table facing the Temple of Saturn. They'll know."

Piazza di Trevi – Early Evening

On her walk back toward the hotel, Selena took a detour.

The streets narrowed, winding through cobbled alleys kissed by jasmine vines and laundry lines. She followed the sound first, a deep, steady roar, like a river against a hollowed stone, and then the light. It reflected off the walls in flickers, hinting at something mythic just around the bend.

Piazza di Trevi opened before her like a hidden theatre, and the fountain at its heart roared like a living god.

Fontana di Trevi. Rome's most dramatic wish-maker. The great sea god Oceanus stood high in the central niche, his marble form commanding, flanked by Tritons wrestling two rearing hippocampi—one wild, one subdued. Water thundered from beneath the chariot, cascading over artificial cliffs in silver torrents. It was theatrical in design, overwhelming in scale, yet somehow still sacred, as if centuries of whispered wishes had sanctified the stone

Tourists crowded its base, coins in hand. Children laughed. A violinist played something slow and aching nearby. Above the din, Selena sensed something older, the weight of centuries in every ripple of that water.

The fountain was completed in 1762, but its spiritual roots stretched back nearly two thousand years. It marked the terminus of the Aqua Virgo, an aqueduct commissioned by Marcus Agrippa in 19 BCE, which once supplied water to the ancient Roman baths and fountains nearby. The very flow that now danced in baroque extravagance had once filled cisterns in the Empire's earliest centuries. It was theatrical in scale, overwhelming in presence, yet somehow sacred. As if the centuries of whispered wishes had sanctified the stone.

She found a quiet table at a wine bar just off the square. The waiter brought her a glass of Montepulciano, deep and dark, still breathing in the glass.

Selena sipped slowly. The noise dulled. The stone beneath her feet felt warm.

And then, as before, the world bent slightly.

....

Dream Trace – The Body as Vow, Rome, Circa 1st Century CE

A Roman villa. Vellichi at its threshold. A scroll in her hem. The weight of ritual. The moment before betrayal.

The vision flared, then disappeared again, leaving behind only her quickened breath and the metallic taste of memory.

She reached for her notebook and jotted a single sentence.

She was the message. The vow was embedded in her body.

She continued sipping her wine and absorbing the atmosphere before she stood when the glass was empty. She left a few coins including tips, nodded her thanks with a big smile to the waiter, and made her way slowly back toward the Forum.

....

Hotel Forum – Rooftop Dinner

Her room welcomed her like a cloak at the end of a long day. The shutters were open. The sky had begun to bruise into evening, and the golden stone of the Forum below had taken on a quieter tone, as if the ruins themselves had begun to dream. Selena freshened up, washing her face with cool water and letting the scent of her travel-stained clothes be replaced by lavender soap and linen. She changed into a fresh wrap dress.

The rooftop of Hotel Forum was already half full when Selena arrived, the evening air still warm but softened by the breeze rising off the old stones below. The waiter, recognising her name, led her straight to a reserved table near the terrace railing.

The Temple of Saturn stood just beyond, its seven columns silhouetted in gold light, the broken marble glowing faintly like bones under skin. Somewhere down in the Forum, a flute player played something slow and shapeless, barely audible above the gentle clinking of cutlery and wine glasses.

Matteo stood as she approached. He had changed into a charcoal jacket over his linen shirt, sleeves rolled again but now paired with a well-worn leather watchstrap. His posture, as always, was one of quiet observance, less a man holding court, more a man taking notes at one.

"You were right," Selena said, sliding into her seat, "the view is ridiculous."

He smiled. "Rome doesn't do subtle well."

The waiter poured wine, a Chianti Riserva, deep and garnet-dark and left the bottle without a word. They sat in comfortable silence for a few moments, watching the light recede from the rooftops across the city, where satellite dishes perched beside domes and doves.

"So," Matteo said, tilting his glass, "what did you make of the inscription?"

Selena traced the rim of her glass slowly before answering. "It's not a trade tag. That much is clear. It reads like a message, personal, coded. Something passed between hands that weren't supposed to be seen touching."

He nodded, pleased. "I thought you'd catch that. Most assume it's a fragment of a ledger. I disagree. The phrasing—'by vow'—isn't commercial. It's devotional. Possibly even esoteric."

"Have you seen others like it?"

"Not many. But fragments, yes. There's a copper scroll found in Alexandria, 1892. It mentions a 'sisterhood of fire-bearers from the ports of the East.' The link was dismissed as poetic invention. But now, with this inscription from Ostia..." He trailed off.

"You think it's part of a larger network," Selena said.

"I do. And you're not the only one. There's a small circle of us trying to draw those lines. Trade wasn't just goods. It was cosmology. Ceremony. Transmission of rites across sea routes. Pepper might have paid the toll, but something else always travelled with it."

Matteo refilled both their glasses, the Chianti catching the candlelight in its ruby depths. "You've walked this path before, haven't you?" he said, almost as a musing rather than a question. "Not literally. Something older than that."

Selena didn't answer immediately. She let the breeze speak first, rustling the napkins, nudging the flame. Then she met his eyes.

"I listen," she said softly. "Some places speak through stone. Others through absence. Rome doesn't whisper, it waits."

He studied her for a moment, then nodded, as if recognising something not quite nameable. "Some truths don't arrive by logic. They rise like smoke. Familiar before they're understood."

Their food arrived, roasted sea bass over fennel, and a plate of braised chicory with lemon and anchovy. Matteo asked no further questions for several minutes, as if to let the moment breathe. Below them, the city dimmed further, turning from stone to shadow.

When he finally spoke again, it was quieter.

"There's a mosaic you should see. At Palazzo Massimo. It's not on display, but I can arrange access. It was found under a collapsed villa near Pompeii. A dancer, arms lifted in an unmistakable gesture. The stance, one arm raised, one lowered, isn't Roman. Not entirely. I've seen it once before."

Selena didn't need to ask where.

She nodded, pulse steady. "I'll go tomorrow."

He lifted his glass. "To memory. However it finds us."

Selena touched her glass to his. The clink rang clear into the night.

Hotel Forum – Post Dinner Meditation

Back in her room, the evening air was turning cooler, but Selena didn't close the shutters. The Forum below glowed in low amber light, ancient stone softened into silhouette. Voices echoed faintly from the street below, glasses clinking, the call of a street performer tuning a harp, footsteps on worn marble.

Selena dimmed the bedside lamp and sat on her bed facing the seal. The seal rested at end of the bed. She lit the wick of a tealight which was on the cabinet in front of her and let the flame steady.

Then she sat, spine aligned, legs folded. The stillness came quickly.

Something within her stirred. Not a rise, not yet but a hum beneath the surface. As if the energy that lived dormant in the base of her spine had begun to notice her noticing it. A quiet prelude to something larger. Her chakras didn't light, they listened.

Tonight, it surged.

A pulsing rhythm unfurled at the base of her spine. Her root chakra glowed hot and red in her inner field, anchoring her to earth. Then the warmth lifted; sacral, solar plexus, heart, each opening like a lantern behind her ribs. The flame climbed further, throat, third eye, crown, until all seven centres thrummed like strings of a single lyre.

The energy didn't spiral. It wove.

It was not a ladder to climb. It was a circuit reconnecting itself. A message preparing to land.

Her hands moved unconsciously, palms open and turned upward. Her breath slowed, lips parted.

A whisper inside her skull:

You are the vessel, not the vault. She remembers through you.

And then, the candle flickered.

Her vision darkened.

....

Dream Trace – Under the Lion's Gaze, Rome, Circa 1st Century CE (Vellichi's Perspective)

The lion statue's paw was cool beneath her fingers. Amber-eyed, silent. Watching.

Vellichi stood in the outer portico of Villa Cassiana, cloaked in silk dyed from crushed madder root. Her jewellery was modest by Roman standards, but every piece had meaning, amulets encoded with sacred geometry, beads anointed with temple oil.

A scroll was stitched into the lining of her sash. Inked in a blend of Tamil siddham and Chaldean star charts, it held not only knowledge but initiation. Sacred correspondences between sky and body. Breath and fire.

It was meant for Senator Flavius Cassianus, known for his Eastern affiliations and interest in arcane rites. A man with influence over Rome's maritime policies. But Vellichi knew influence was never clean.

She waited until the moon arched over the broken column above the aqueduct, a sign. Then entered.

Inside, the villa glittered with excess. Red-veined marble. Hanging lamps. Musicians tuning lyres by the fountain.

But Vellichi saw the dancers. Three of them.

One Roman, one Nubian, one from Anatolia. Their movements echoed her own lineage, shoulders rolling, arms carved into flame. They danced not for entertainment, but invocation.

"The body knows what empires forget."

The phrase pulsed in her ribs.

Then, betrayal. Subtle. Fast.

A servant, too pale for the kitchen, too alert for the background; stepped between her and the senator's door. He smiled with the cold efficiency of someone who already knew what she carried. Her seal was demanded. Her scroll intercepted. Her name twisted into accusation.

Vellichi didn't resist. Not because she was weak. Because she had seen this before. In a vision from a temple in Egypt where Tamil, Nubian, and Hellenic priestesses once trained together in mirrored chambers. Where a high priestess in lapis blue had said:

"What your people call Deva-dasi, we once knew as well. The body as offering. The dance as scripture. The voice as portal. The Empire forgets. The body remembers."

Even as guards escorted her away, Vellichi turned to the lion statue at the portico.

Its amber eyes met hers.

Not pity. Not warning.

Memory.

The city didn't just remember her
it was waiting for her answer.

Selena's Diary Entry

Field Notes – Museo Nazionale Romano, Rome (Palazzo Altemps, Research Days 1–2)

Mission:

Uncover Tamil–Roman ceremonial and cosmological overlaps embedded in trade inscriptions and temple art. Examine encoded feminine transmission—via dance, scroll, or vow. Begin tracing Vellichi's presence in Rome and the interrupted covenant between emissary and senator. Reconstruct the body-memory of sacred performers across empires.

Chakra Thread:

Heart Chakra Opening — emotional release of sacred betrayal across lifetimes

Crown + Root Activation — gravitational alignment between earth legacy and divine recall

Early Kundalini Flare — pre-awakening hum; awareness of chakra circuit and energetic imprint from relics

Keywords:

- Tamil–Roman trade (Muziris–Ostia axis)
- Devadasi / courtesan-priestess cross-pollination
- "The keeper of the flame" as spiritual lineage figure
- Sacred vows disguised as diplomatic messages
- Dream memory flare: scroll, betrayal, lion statue, seal
- Vellichi as emissary of hidden rites
  - **Onyx seal — மெய் ("truth")**
- Palimpsest cities / mirrored sanctuaries

- "The body knows what empires forget.
- "Flavius Cassianus (fictional composite: trade–mystery Senate ally)
- Matteo Ferini — memory-mirroring scholar, dream seer
- Unfulfilled rites, fragmented sisterhoods
- The mosaic of the dancer — Pompeii as conduit of Tamil rite-memory
- Encoded ritual as survival through collapse

Chapter Twelve –
The Veins of Isis

Alexandria, Egypt – Present Day

The sea shimmered as if it held memory in its tide. Selena stood on the narrow balcony of the Cecil Hotel, its wrought-iron balustrade warm beneath her fingertips, sun-kissed from the day. A soft breeze tugged at the hem of her linen shirt, bringing with it the scent of brine, engine smoke, and cardamom-sweet tea from the cafés along Saad Zaghloul Street.

Below, the Eastern Harbour murmured in its own layered language, masts clinking like wind chimes, gulls wheeling above flat-roofed buildings, and the low thrum of scooters weaving between rusted taxis. Merchants called out in Arabic, French, and the occasional fragment of Italian, their voices rising and falling like sea-songs echoing through the alleyways.

Alexandria pulsed with history, but not quietly. It exhaled it in every stone and shadow. Just blocks away stood the site of the ancient Library of Alexandria, where scrolls once burned and secrets vanished. Now, the modern Bibliotheca Alexandrina rose like a sun disk etched with languages from across the world, an ode, not a replacement.

The Cecil Hotel itself was no stranger to forgotten empires. Built in 1929 on land once home to a royal palace, it had hosted kings, spies, poets, and presidents. Agatha Christie had reportedly stayed here. Churchill and Montgomery too. Its corridors still carried the scent of polished brass and dusted velvet, and the ceilings were etched with colonial ambition, Art Deco chandeliers dangling like relics of a time both gilded and gone. From her room, Selena could almost see the silhouettes of British officers lingering in the lounge, cigars in hand, unaware that beneath their boots lay centuries of deeper, older magic.

She had arrived in Alexandria that morning, barely twenty-four hours after rereading Matteo's note.

The copper scroll. 1892. Alexandria.

It wasn't a breadcrumb.

It was a summons.

Her steps felt guided now, not just by curiosity, but by something more physical. Like muscle remembering a ritual. Like skin responding to sun.

"From the pepper port, by vow, to the keeper of the flame."

The words weren't done with her.

And neither was Alexandria.

Bibliotheca Alexandrina – Archives Room, Afternoon

The library was a marvel of modern architecture, angled glass panes and slanted granite façades curving like sails mid-horizon. Light poured through the tilted roof in long golden bands, illuminating the stone carvings of alphabets from every language known to human history. It was built to reflect the dream of the original Library of Alexandria, a beacon of knowledge lost to fire, now reborn in glass and intention.

But the real story was downstairs.

Selena descended into the restricted archives, escorted by a silent attendant, her ID badge clipped to her blouse. The subterranean level smelled of pressed paper, cedar polish, and dust held in suspension. Every corridor whispered.

Dr Layla Saad greeted her near a temperature-controlled reading alcove, dressed in charcoal robes threaded with copper embroidery, her frame stately but soft. A silver pendant shaped like the Eye of Horus rested just above her collarbone. Her expression was reserved, professional but something in her eyes hinted at measured curiosity.

Dr Layla was a historian of Egyptian esoteric traditions and comparative script systems, with a doctorate from the Université Paris-Sorbonne and a joint fellowship at the Institute for Ancient Civilisations in Luxor. Selena had been introduced to her through Dr Suresh, her mentor in Chennai and a scholar of ancient Indian inscriptions. A single email, part academic, part intuitive plea, had secured the meeting.

"I must say, your request was... unconventional," Layla said, gesturing to the reading table already prepared. "But Suresh's name carries weight. He's an old friend."

"This copy," Layla continued, laying out a preserved folio from the 1892 expedition, "was transcribed by a German Orientalist. The original is kept in our vault, unrepaired. Too delicate for display."

Selena leaned over the vellum. Copper-toned ink spiralled across the page, Tamil-Brahmi curving into angular Demotic, separated by delicate lines that looked more like talismans than punctuation.

"By seal and vow, we carry flame through trade and time. From east of the lion gate to the temple of the hawk-eyed goddess, we remember."

Selena traced the letters gently with her eyes.

"Do you know what the lion gate refers to?" Selena asked, more like accidentally spoke out her mind's voice.

Layla tilted her head. "It could be Mycenae. Or perhaps the Lion Gate at Uraiyur, ancient Chola capital. That's your expertise, not mine."

But Selena noticed the hesitation. The way her fingers stopped just short of the edge of the parchment. She was holding something back.

"What about the triple spiral symbol?" Selena pressed, pointing to a faint etching in the corner.

Layla's hand froze mid-air. "That symbol predates the text. Celtic, Anatolian... and yes, Egyptian. It's been found carved into temple walls dedicated to feminine rites, especially near the catacombs of Kom el-Shoqafa."

She folded her arms, tone growing cautious.

"Some believe Alexandria was founded not only as a port, but as a storehouse. Alexander the Great didn't just dream of empire. He dreamt of knowledge as conquest. The original library was meant to hold every scroll from every port his ships touched, including ones written by emissaries no one dared name."

Selena felt it then, that tightening behind her ribs. The sensation that a page was about to turn inside her own body.

Dr Layla checked the time on her slender watch, then looked up. "Take your time. I've left the scans and notes beside the original folio. I'll give you privacy."

"Thank you," Selena said softly.

Layla nodded and exited with a whisper of cloth and sandals.

Selena sat alone now, just her, the scroll, and the scent of something ancient breaking open.

She hadn't even closed her eyes before it began. The flicker. The weightless pull.

Dream Trace was not a ritual. It was a return.

....

Dream Trace – Vellichi's Arrival, Egypt, Circa 1st Century CE

The felucca glided silently down the Nile, its single white sail catching the breath of dusk like a prayer mid-flight. The river shimmered in bronze and indigo, reflecting not just the sky, but the memory of ancient things. Reeds rustled along the banks. Water lapped gently at the hull in a rhythm older than empire.

At the bow stood Vellichi, wrapped in layers of indigo-dyed silk, her hair braided with copper thread. The breeze carried the scent of river clay, crushed hibiscus, and the spiced trace of myrrh from her wrists. Her fingers, ink-stained from ritual preparation, curled lightly around the hem of her robe, where the scroll, inked with Tamil siddham and Hermetic star glyphs, was stitched into the lining like a concealed organ.

The felucca moored near Kom Ombo, its wood creaking softly against stone. Her sandaled feet sank slightly into the sun-warmed earth, still holding the day's heat. The air was thick with the mingled perfume of jasmine and frankincense, drifting from unseen altars along the path.

135

At the edge of the dunes stood Neferka, waiting.

The sky behind her flared in desert gold and deep garnet. She was tall and serene, her skin like polished obsidian, her robes woven with strands of lapis and bronze. Her kohl-lined eyes did not blink.

They bowed to each other in the ritual greeting of temple kin, palms pressed lightly to chest, breath held for a single beat, heads inclined to the left. It was not submission, but synchrony. The breath before the vow.

"Vellichi," Neferka said in flowing Tamil, each syllable formed with the lilt of sacred cadence. "You've crossed well. The tide did not forget you."

Vellichi smiled, her reply shaped in careful Middle Egyptian, the cadence slow but anchored in respect. "The hawk guides. The lion guards."

They embraced. Not as travellers, but as kin, sisters once initiated in a mirror-chambered sanctuary near the Red Sea, where Tamil, Nubian, and Hellenic rites had once danced in mirrored firelight. Their training had fused calendars, mythologies, and marrow.

Together, they approached the Temple of Isis.

Built during the Ptolemaic Dynasty around the 3rd century BCE and later expanded under the Roman emperors, the Temple of Isis at Philae had become one of the last active sanctuaries of ancient Egyptian religion. Though Alexandria held temples in her honour, it was Philae, an island temple far to the south that preserved her full rites. Here, however, within Kom Ombo's sacred complex, a smaller shrine dedicated to Isis the Navigator, the Mourner, the Restorer of the Body held court near the river's bend. The temple rose from the sandstone like an incantation made solid, its pylons carved with reliefs of birthing goddesses and winged protectors, its inner sanctum whispered over by centuries of priests and initiates. Built not by one king but by generations, Ptolemaic rulers, Roman governors, and unnamed patrons of the Isis cult, the temple served as both spiritual sanctuary and esoteric school, a place where rituals of death and rebirth, astronomical rites, and mystery teachings intertwined. Pilgrims, sailors, and priestesses once travelled from ports across the Mediterranean to offer devotion at her altar, believing Isis could guide the dead through the underworld and the living across uncertain seas. Even now, Vellichi could feel the lingering charge in the air, the sacred residue of offerings burned, vows whispered, truths veiled in allegory. The temple didn't just stand. It remembered.

The colonnades loomed high, their carved capitals alive with shadows. Inside, the air was cool and dense, filled with the resinous smoke of sandalwood, the faint trace of sacred oils rubbed into every crack of stone. Priestesses of varied descent, Tamil, Anatolian, Nubian, all stood barefoot on alabaster floors that held the chill of buried rivers. Gold-tipped torches hissed in sconces. Painted lotus motifs unfurled across the walls like memory in bloom. Winged thrones and serpent crowns watched silently from above.

The rites had already begun.

Each sister stepped forward with her offering, a vial of sacred oil, a chant drawn from three tongues, a mudra carved into air with fingers that had traced constellations.

Vellichi stepped to the altar.

From her robe, she drew the scroll, her breath steady, her hands trembling only slightly as she placed it upon the black stone, now warm from earlier flames. The scroll's edges fluttered, sensing proximity to its destination.

Behind the shrine, the temple flame flared, tall and unwavering.

A low hum began in the room, not a sound, but a vibration, as if memory itself had awakened, stirred by the arrival of something it had once known by heart.

....

Alexandria – Wellness Centre Near Kom el-Dikka – Present Day

Selena hadn't planned on visiting a wellness centre. But after an intense afternoon at the Bibliotheca Alexandrina, she'd found herself sharing tea and lentil soup with Mira Hassan, Dr Layla's junior researcher and archivist-in-training. Young, intuitive, with a sharp mind hidden behind an easy laugh, Mira had been helping catalogue fragments from the same expedition that unearthed the copper scroll. Over dinner, their conversation had veered from scriptwork to sensation.

"You look like someone carrying too much knowing in one body," Mira had said, half-joking, but not entirely. "Before you leave, go see Zeinab. She leads resonance meditations just outside the city centre. It's not on the tourist path. But the ground there holds something."

Selena had raised an eyebrow. "Something?"

"Old heat," Mira replied. "Ritual memory. You'll understand when you feel it."

So, with nothing more than a name and a pin on a map, Selena had gone.

The centre was discreet, built atop partially excavated ruins known only to local scholars and intuitives. Inside, the

Resonance Room felt both ancient and clean: whitewashed walls, copper bowls on shelves, rugs woven in desert tones. The floor was warm underfoot. The ceiling curved softly, sound travelling in round, honeyed echoes.

The air smelled of rose, lime blossom, and aged wood.

Zeinab, the guide, was in her sixties with silver-plaited hair and sun-scorched skin. Her voice was steady. "You may feel warmth. You may feel something more."

Selena stepped barefoot into the giant singing bowl at the centre of the room. It rose to her knees in height, bronze hammered and smooth.

Zeinab tapped the rim.

The sound surged up through her soles like liquid fire.

Again. Another strike. A deeper pitch.

The vibration moved through her legs, into her hips, and anchored at her root chakra, a hot, pulsing centre, as if the bowl had cracked open the earth beneath her.

She gasped. Not from pain. From recognition.

You are remembering with your bones.

She stepped out, unsteady, and knelt in the meditation corner.

Zeinab offered a copper cup of rose water. "Now hum."

Selena closed her eyes. Inhale. One word per breath with the right tone.

"Lam." Root

"Vam." Sacral

"Ram." Solar

"Yam." Heart

"Ham." Throat

"Sham." Third Eye

"Om." Crown

Each sound cracked something open. And then wove it back together. It was magic.

Later that evening, back in her hotel room, Selena unfolded the leaflet Zeinab had handed out at the session, a simple page with seven chakra symbols and their associated bija mantras. A key for inner architecture.

She sat cross-legged on the floor facing the ocean, lit a tealight, the sea wind whispering against the balcony shutters, and began to chant softly. Each syllable vibrated differently in her body: LAM settled in her spine like a red ember, VAM spiralled through her pelvis, RAM sparked above her navel. The energy didn't just rise, it flowed, one centre igniting the next like lanterns strung on an ancient path.

With every repetition, she felt not only more awake, but more remembered. As if this practice wasn't something she was learning, but something she was returning to.

She would continue this ritual in the days to come. The mantras weren't sounds. They were keys.

Flash Memory – Palazzo Massimo, Rome

Three days before flying to Alexandria, Selena had arrived at Palazzo Massimo alle Terme, tucked just north of Termini Station, a stone's throw from the Baths of Diocletian. The façade was stately, neoclassical, graceful symmetry in travertine and ochre, once a Jesuit boarding school, now the quiet heart of Roman antiquities.

The air inside was cool and dry, infused with the scent of old marble, beeswax polish, and time. Polished wooden floors hushed footfalls. Arched ceilings towered above her like a held breath. Columns framed frescoed rooms where light filtered through tall windows like water through silk.

The elevator had taken her down, two levels below the public galleries into the restricted mosaic vault, where temperature and humidity were tightly monitored. The door was marked with no signage, just a bronze plaque and a silent keycard panel.

There she had met Dr Franco Verani.

He stood tall, lean, perhaps in his early fifties, with ash-brown curls peppered at the temples and reading glasses tucked into his collar. His linen shirt was the colour of bleached bone, sleeves rolled up to the elbows. An archaeologist by training, archivist by temperament, he had a voice like polished gravel and a gaze that moved slower than most, as if measuring time across multiple scales.

"I owe Matteo more than one favour," he'd said as he welcomed her in. "He said you were looking for patterns hidden beneath stone. I thought this might qualify."

They walked together down a narrow aisle lit only by indirect LEDs. The walls glowed with tesserae, tiny, coloured tiles set centuries ago by hands that understood beauty as a sacred task.

At the far end, sealed behind a glass panel, was a mosaic fragment recovered from a collapsed villa near Pompeii.

The image struck like thunder.

A dancer. Mid-motion. Barefoot on a ring of stylised lotus petals. Her arms extended in a stance unmistakable to anyone who had ever studied classical Tamil iconography.

One arm lifted, palm out, protection.

The other lowered, fingers turned toward the earth, blessing.

Abhaya. Varada. The gesture of Durga.

"She's not Roman," Luca had whispered. "Not entirely. Some archaeologists argue she mirrors the Tamil goddess Durga; warrior, protector, destroyer of illusion. A Chola connection. There are shipping records from Puteoli that mention temple dancers arriving from the East. Some believe these images were devotional imports. Carried by emissaries. Or buried by them."

Selena had barely heard him. Her eyes locked on the tile work, lapis, terracotta, bone white, gold. Her hand moved without thinking, rising toward the glass.

Her fingers hovered before the dancer's outstretched palm.

And then, her own arm lifted, not consciously, not performatively, but in echo.

A gesture remembered.

The line between posture and prayer blurred.

Reflections on the Maritime Silk Road

Selena sat now in the quiet of her hotel room in Alexandria, journal open.

The sea, Rome, Egypt. The triple spiral. Vellichi. Devadasis and Wabet priestesses. The mosaic dancer. The copper scroll.

This wasn't trade.

It was transmission.

The Maritime Silk Road hadn't only moved spices and gold.

It had moved cosmologies.

Long before maps were drawn with borders, they were shaped by tides. Tamil ships laden with pepper, pearls, and

142

sandalwood met Roman vessels off the coast of Muziris. Egyptian scribes in Berenike recorded gifts from the "Land of the Moon." Chinese silk, Southeast Asian incense, and Indian cotton passed through Red Sea ports like Quseir and Myos Hormos. But alongside cargo, something subtler moved; chants memorised, rituals shared, gods renamed, rites re-rooted.

Temple dancers became emissaries. Scrolls encoded with Vedic and Hermetic correspondences changed hands in silence. Sacred oils blended across languages. Ritual gestures slipped across seas, taking root in temples far from their origin. The Maritime Silk Road was not just commerce, it was choreography.

Feminine rites disguised as diplomacy.

Sacred knowledge encrypted in trade.

The world had forgotten.

Her body hadn't.

In the silence of the temple's heart,
her name returned to her,
not the one she was born with,
but the one she vowed to protect.

Selena's Diary Entry

Field Notes – Alexandria, Egypt (Day 1–2)

Mission:

Trace the esoteric transmissions embedded in Tamil–Egyptian maritime exchange. Decode ritual scrolls from the 1892 copper scroll expedition. Confirm the presence of feminine rites disguised in trade and temple records. Uncover Vellichi's role within the Temple of Isis sisterhood and the symbolic resonance between Alexandria, Rome, and Muziris.

Chakra Thread:

Root Chakra ignition – Kundalini begins with memory encoded in bone

Heart + Crown Expansion – emotional clarity and metaphysical awakening

Full chakra linkage through mantra: LAM → OM — the circuit lights

Phrases:

"You are remembering with your bones."

"Her name returned... not the one she was born with, but the one she vowed to protect."

"From east of the lion gate to the temple of the hawk-eyed goddess..."

Keywords:

- Kom Ombo / Temple of Isis / sacred maritime crossings
- Triple spiral symbol – feminine rite of cyclical knowledge
- Tamil siddham + Hermetic cipher fusion

- Zeinab's resonance bowl & the bija mantra key
- Dream Trace — Vellichi & Neferka / shared temple lineage
- Temple dancers = emissaries of cosmology
- Devadasis, Wabet priestesses, and Chola-Alexandrian rites
- Durga mosaic, Pompeii / Chola-Roman connection
- The Silk Road as choreography, not just commerce
- Transmission through the body: postures, breath, chant

Chapter Thirteen –
A River That Speaks

Nile Delta, Egypt – Present Day

The Nile curved like a hymn across the earth, its waters older than maps, older than memory.

Selena had arrived at the Delta just before noon. The journey from Alexandria took nearly three hours, following the western edge of the Rosetta branch, where the Nile began to unspool itself into the arms of the Mediterranean. Mira had arranged the transport; a battered white Peugeot driven by an elderly man named Fathi, whose weathered hands held the steering wheel like a prayer bead. He spoke little English, but his smile was kind and his driving patient.

As they passed through the edge of Rashid, Selena watched the land unfold like a scroll; canals glinting under sun, flooded fields dense with sugarcane and rice, buffaloes bathing shoulder-deep in muddy ditches. Boys flew kites from rooftops. Women in headscarves rinsed clothes in the shallows. Wooden boats rocked gently beside date palms.

The smell of the delta was layered; river silt and sun-warmed stone, jasmine, old diesel, ripe tomatoes, and distant smoke. The air carried it all.

The Nile Delta had always been more than a river mouth. To ancient Egyptians, it was the mouth of life. The green cradle that fed the empire, both physically and cosmologically. The pharaohs called it Sekhet-Aaru, the Fields of Reeds, where souls passed into the afterlife if their hearts were found lighter than a feather.

Culturally, it had been a great mingler. Upper and Lower Egypt found their unity here. Priests, merchants, and emissaries sailed down from Thebes and up from Memphis, anchoring in river ports where gods changed names and languages blurred. Cleopatra, it was said, once floated through the Delta on a golden barge with purple sails, her perfume wafting to the shore before the oars even touched water.

In political times, the Delta was a shield, buffering Egypt from sea-bound invasion. In spiritual terms, it was a mirror of the heavens. Many temples had been aligned with the stars, designed so the sun would rise directly between their pylons at equinox.

Now, in modern times, the Nile Delta was quieter but no less vital. Cell towers punctuated the skyline beside minarets. Farmers bartered bags of lentils beside glassy phone stalls. Rusted bicycles leaned against ancient stone wells. Some ruins stood buried beneath cane fields. Others waited to be found.

Fathi dropped her off near an irrigation path where the road ended and the earth softened underfoot. A local field hand pointed her wordlessly toward a thicket of reeds and uneven stones.

She walked alone now, boots trailing clay, guided by symbols and memory: a spiral noted in a German journal from 1896; an inscription from the copper scroll that referenced a "temple swallowed by sand where the lioness once drank."

Here, the Nile widened and grew still. No motors. No noise. Just birds calling through the reeds and the wind shaping the water like breath.

She reached the embankment and paused.

There. Half-submerged in mud and shadow, a stretch of carved limestone wall jutted from the riverbank. Eroded, cracked but unmistakably shaped by human hands. Along its surface; a single, unbroken glyph.

A serpent coiled through a lotus bloom.

Selena's breath caught.

She had seen that symbol only in dreams.

She dropped to her knees beside it, fingertips brushing mud from the etched lines. Her heart beat in slow, deep strikes, like oars through water.

This place had been buried for centuries. But now, uncovered by storm, or tide, or timing....it called to her.

She sat back on her heels, mud coating her palms. The sun above her had turned the reeds to gold. The air shimmered with heat. Something ancient was rising; not from the land, but from within her.

She closed her eyes.

The heat behind her ribs deepened. Her spine aligned instinctively. Breath slowed.

The Delta was quiet.

But below the silence: a hum.

The line between waking and dreaming dissolved, not like sleep, but like a tide withdrawing from the shore. A space opened in her mind, wide and waiting.

And then.....like silk unraveling, she slipped.

Backward, inward.

Toward a crossing she hadn't yet made.

....

Dream Trace – Vellichi's Final Crossing, Red Sea Port, Circa 1st Century CE

The heat hit her first.

Not the brittle sun of desert noon, but a deeper warmth — the kind that came from stone walls still holding fire, from sand that had known rituals, from a sky so wide it rang like a bell.

Vellichi opened her eyes.

Or someone did.

Her feet were already moving, bare and dust-caked, sandals tucked into the fold of her girdled robe. Her braid swung heavily against her back, threaded with copper coins and pieces of jet. A gold seal-ring pressed warm against her middle finger, the one etched with the serpent coiled through lotus.

She stood at the edge of a Red Sea inlet, the salt air coiling around her like a veil.

Behind her, the old spice road wound into the cliffs. Before her, the port of Berenike shimmered under the lowering sun, a half-buried jewel of warehouses, shrines, and watchtowers carved into red rock. Roman soldiers moved like shadows along the colonnades, but the heart of the port was not theirs.

It belonged to those who moved between languages, between borders, between gods.

Tamil, Kushite, Nabataean. Women with sacred ink beneath their fingernails. Traders who carried maps in their bones. Midwives of memory.

She crossed the stone platform that once served as a docking altar. Below, dhows were moored; curved wooden ships bearing palm cargo, amulets, scrolls. Incense drifted from a nearby firepit: sandalwood, frankincense, and a trace of blue lotus.

She knew the path by heart.

Past the collapsed tower where the old moon temple once stood. Past the cistern that caught monsoon rain. Toward a grove of tamarisk trees, where the temple stood.

Not a grand temple. A hidden one.

Built from local stone and coral brick. A place not marked on any map, only named in vow:

Alaya Varahi. The Temple of the Primordial Flame.

She entered through the low threshold.

Inside, the air was cooler. Still. Thick with histories not spoken aloud. A set of steps led downward into a sanctum only lit by the open ceiling above; where the desert sun slanted in, dividing light from shadow in perfect symmetry.

There were three others waiting.

A Kushite initiate wearing a girdle of white shells.

A Greek priestess, her head shaved, her hands marked with blue ink.

And Neferka.

Older now, her braids wrapped in lapis cloth, her stance unshaken.

Vellichi nodded.

No words were exchanged. Only breath.

She stepped to the center of the chamber, where a shallow basin of red clay stood waiting. She knelt, unfastened the hem of her robe, and pulled the final scroll from its stitched lining.

The parchment trembled slightly in her hands, as if recognising its destination.

Etched in overlapping systems; Tamil siddham, Demotic glyphs, and star-mapped sigils, it was not a scroll of theology or trade. It was a convergence. A guide to sacred motion, breath, herbal correspondences, stellar alignments, and energy thresholds.

The priestess from Ionia began a chant. A sound that was not quite sung, more remembered.

Vellichi added her voice to it. The vibration filled the chamber. The serpent-lotus seal on her ring warmed, then flared with light.

They did not burn the scroll.

They buried it.

Wrapped in oiled linen and placed beneath the basin; sealed with salt, obsidian, and a single drop of each woman's blood. They covered it with sand from the altar floor, marking the spot with a triple spiral carved into the rim of the basin stone.

Then, they waited.

Hours later, the storm came, wild and unexpected. The sky turned copper. Wind screamed through the canyon like a warning. Sand poured through the temple's roof, burying the floor in minutes.

Vellichi stood still, the dust clinging to her lashes, arms open wide in invocation.

"This is not loss," she whispered in Tamil.

"This is remembrance sealed in earth."

And then—

Nothing but silence.

And the wind howling over what was no longer seen.

....

The Temple Uncovered, Red Sea Foothills, Midday Heat – Present Day

The desert wind had shifted sometime before dawn, leaving a fine crust of silt on the expedition tents. Selena stood beside a cluster of surveyors as the sun climbed higher, its white heat bouncing off rock and tarp. The dig site looked unremarkable at first; half-eroded, bone-dry stone walls buried beneath windblown sand. But the glyphs changed everything.

They had emerged only after a freak flash flood swept through the wadi days earlier, revealing the curvature of temple walls, inscriptions half-buried, but unmistakable, serpent entwined with lotus, coiled in a protective spiral. The very symbol that had haunted Selena's dreams since Rome.

The archaeological team was cautious. The site was undocumented, its foundation style pre-Ptolemaic, but the iconography hinted at syncretic rites; Tamil, Egyptian, even Hellenistic. One wall bore a carving of a woman standing in a flame halo, arms extended in dual gesture; protection and release. Another, a stylised map with sea routes running eastward, marked by stars.

Selena knelt, brushing sand from a line of glyphs still slick with moisture. Her breath caught. These weren't just devotional, they were directional. Coordinates encoded in prayer.

"He believed in empire by intellect."

Dr Layla's voice echoed in her mind, a conversation shared back in Alexandria.

"Alexander didn't come to Egypt just to rule it. He came to build something eternal. That's why he founded Alexandria;

not just a city, but a portal. His legacy was not just conquest, but curation. Knowledge itself was his monument."

Selena could see it now. This temple tucked between land and sea, marked by fire and water, was not a site of worship alone. It was a sanctuary for transmission. The kind Alexander dreamed of preserving through scrolls, languages, emissaries.

And perhaps, it had never been lost; only waiting for the right current to lift the sand.

She turned toward the rising wind and felt something loosen inside her chest. Not a revelation.

A remembering.

The Letter, Guesthouse by the Red Sea – Dusk

The guesthouse was quiet, its sandstone walls warmed by the day's sun, now blushing rose under the fading light. The building itself was old; a converted Ottoman caravanserai perched just above the shoreline near Marsa Alam, its stone floors cooled by evening breezes and the low hum of ceiling fans. Jasmine vines crawled up one wall. A brass lantern flickered gently beside the writing desk.

Selena sat at the window with her journal open, the smell of salt and sandalwood clinging to her sleeves. Outside, the tide crept in slowly, a hush against the reef.

She dipped her pen in ink.

This letter wasn't to anyone she could name. Not Matteo. Not Layla. Not even Vellichi.

This was to the sea.

To time.

To memory itself.

"You were never silent.

You were waiting.
For someone who could listen with their bones.
I vow not to steal your stories.
I vow to carry them forward.
As flame.
As breath.
As dance."

A single wave broke loudly on the shore. She paused, letting the echo root itself in her ribs.

"This isn't research anymore.
It's return."

She placed the pen down gently.

Outside, the night had arrived quietly. The stars blinked like old eyes waking up.

And from the sea below, something answered.

Not in words.

But in warmth.

Like a vow accepted.

Reflections on the Lost Port

Selena stood on the ridge overlooking the excavation site just beyond the modern coast; a windswept plain of broken stone and salt-bitten silence. Beneath her feet lay the bones of Berenike, once a vital Red Sea port under Ptolemaic and Roman control, now crumbling into the sand like half-remembered scripture. Once, elephants bound for the imperial arenas of Rome were offloaded here. Once, Tamil spices, Nubian incense, and Persian textiles passed through the stone gates like offerings to time. Once, the sacred and the practical braided themselves into the rhythm of dockside ritual.

Even now, the remains of temple walls, votive niches, and storerooms clung to the landscape, whispering of their former purpose. Archaeologists had unearthed inscriptions in Tamil-Brahmi, Hellenic, and Demotic; unlikely siblings sharing the same breath. Clay amulets shaped like lotuses and serpents, shards of ritual vessels, fragments of star charts, all hinted that this had not merely been a trade station. It had been a threshold, a place of convergence between material exchange and spiritual transmission.

The air smelled of dust, salt, and iron; clean, sharp, ancient. Wind curled through the arches of partially revealed structures, playing melodies against stone like a forgotten reed instrument. In the distance, the Red Sea shimmered, unwavering, like a mirror held between worlds.

Selena closed her eyes, pressing her palm to the serpent-lotus seal now carved on a recovered altar slab.

"This was a sanctuary disguised as a port," she thought. "A school of fire-veiled knowledge, hidden in plain sight. They had not lost their wisdom to conquest. They had buried it, so one day, someone like me could find it again."

The temple was never built to be remembered in books.

It was built to be felt in the body.

And her body was finally listening.

A single tear slid down her cheek; not of grief, but recognition.

She wasn't just an archaeologist.

She was the answer the ruins had been waiting for.

Selena's Vow

Beneath the stars, beside the ancient sea, Selena whispered a vow; not to a god, not to a person, but to the land itself.

"I will carry what was meant to move.
I will speak what was once sealed.
I am not merely a seeker.
I am the return."

The wind didn't still.
It bowed.
Selena's circuit was now complete.
From root to crown, she no longer merely remembered.
She now embodied.
She turned from the ruins with the sun behind her. Not everything buried was lost. Some things were simply waiting to be spoken again.

The river never forgot.
It had only been waiting for her voice.

Selena's Diary Entry

Field Notes – Red Sea Guesthouse, Near Marsa Alam

Mission:

Investigate the convergence of Tamil-Chola emissaries with Egyptian temple culture at Berenike. Study seal iconography, trace sacred feminine transmission through trade ports, and identify symbolic language overlaps between Vedic and Hermetic systems.

Chakra Thread:

Root- Anchoring ancestral memory into the physical — the body as the first temple, the land as the ultimate scripture.

Crown- Connection to eternal memory — the cosmos as archive, where sacred knowledge circulates in stars, symbols, and sensation.

Keywords:

- Berenike Port
- Lotus-serpent glyph
- Port as sanctuary
- Fire-veiled rites
- Soul cartography
- Geo-memory
- "The temple was never meant to be known — only remembered"
- Scrolls sewn into silk hems
- Knowledge buried, not lost

Chapter Fourteen –
The Dessert
Remembers

Shiraz, Iran – Present Day

The Nile curved like a hymn across the earth, its waters older than maps, older than memory.

Selena had arrived at the Delta just before noon. The journey from Alexandria took nearly three hours, following the western edge of the Rosetta branch, where the Nile began to unspool itself into the arms of the Mediterranean. Mira had arranged the transport; a battered white Peugeot driven by an elderly man named Fathi, whose weathered hands held the steering wheel like a prayer bead. He spoke little English, but his smile was kind and his driving patient.

As they passed through the edge of Rashid, Selena watched the land unfold like a scroll; canals glinting under sun, flooded fields dense with sugarcane and rice, buffaloes bathing shoulder-deep in muddy ditches. Boys flew kites from rooftops. Women in headscarves rinsed clothes in the shallows. Wooden boats rocked gently beside date palms.

The smell of the delta was layered; river silt and sun-warmed stone, jasmine, old diesel, ripe tomatoes, and distant smoke. The air carried it all.

The Nile Delta had always been more than a river mouth. To ancient Egyptians, it was the mouth of life. The green cradle that fed the empire, both physically and cosmologically. The pharaohs called it Sekhet-Aaru, the Fields of Reeds, where souls passed into the afterlife if their hearts were found lighter than a feather.

Culturally, it had been a great mingler. Upper and Lower Egypt found their unity here. Priests, merchants, and emissaries sailed down from Thebes and up from Memphis, anchoring in river ports where gods changed names and languages blurred. Cleopatra, it was said, once floated through the Delta on a golden barge with purple sails, her perfume wafting to the shore before the oars even touched water.

In political times, the Delta was a shield, buffering Egypt from sea-bound invasion. In spiritual terms, it was a mirror of the heavens. Many temples had been aligned with the stars, designed so the sun would rise directly between their pylons at equinox.

Now, in modern times, the Nile Delta was quieter but no less vital. Cell towers punctuated the skyline beside minarets. Farmers bartered bags of lentils beside glassy phone stalls. Rusted bicycles leaned against ancient stone wells. Some ruins stood buried beneath cane fields. Others waited to be found.

Fathi dropped her off near an irrigation path where the road ended and the earth softened underfoot. A local field hand pointed her wordlessly toward a thicket of reeds and uneven stones.

She walked alone now, boots trailing clay, guided by symbols and memory: a spiral noted in a German journal from

1896; an inscription from the copper scroll that referenced a "temple swallowed by sand where the lioness once drank."

Here, the Nile widened and grew still. No motors. No noise. Just birds calling through the reeds and the wind shaping the water like breath.

She reached the embankment and paused.

There. Half-submerged in mud and shadow, a stretch of carved limestone wall jutted from the riverbank. Eroded, cracked but unmistakably shaped by human hands. Along its surface; a single, unbroken glyph.

A serpent coiled through a lotus bloom.

Selena's breath caught.

She had seen that symbol only in dreams.

She dropped to her knees beside it, fingertips brushing mud from the etched lines. Her heart beat in slow, deep strikes, like oars through water.

This place had been buried for centuries. But now, uncovered by storm, or tide, or timing....it called to her.

She sat back on her heels, mud coating her palms. The sun above her had turned the reeds to gold. The air shimmered with heat. Something ancient was rising; not from the land, but from within her.

She closed her eyes.

The heat behind her ribs deepened. Her spine aligned instinctively. Breath slowed.

The Delta was quiet.

But below the silence: a hum.

The line between waking and dreaming dissolved, not like sleep, but like a tide withdrawing from the shore. A space opened in her mind, wide and waiting.

And then.....like silk unraveling, she slipped.

Backward, inward.

Toward a crossing she hadn't yet made.

....

Dream Trace – Vellichi's Final Crossing, Red Sea Port, Circa 1st Century CE

The heat hit her first.

Not the brittle sun of desert noon, but a deeper warmth — the kind that came from stone walls still holding fire, from sand that had known rituals, from a sky so wide it rang like a bell.

Vellichi opened her eyes.

Or someone did.

Her feet were already moving, bare and dust-caked, sandals tucked into the fold of her girdled robe. Her braid swung heavily against her back, threaded with copper coins and pieces of jet. A gold seal-ring pressed warm against her middle finger, the one etched with the serpent coiled through lotus.

She stood at the edge of a Red Sea inlet, the salt air coiling around her like a veil.

Behind her, the old spice road wound into the cliffs. Before her, the port of Berenike shimmered under the lowering sun, a half-buried jewel of warehouses, shrines, and watchtowers carved into red rock. Roman soldiers moved like shadows along the colonnades, but the heart of the port was not theirs.

It belonged to those who moved between languages, between borders, between gods.

Tamil, Kushite, Nabataean. Women with sacred ink beneath their fingernails. Traders who carried maps in their bones. Midwives of memory.

She crossed the stone platform that once served as a docking altar. Below, dhows were moored; curved wooden ships bearing palm cargo, amulets, scrolls. Incense drifted from a nearby firepit: sandalwood, frankincense, and a trace of blue lotus.

She knew the path by heart.

Past the collapsed tower where the old moon temple once stood. Past the cistern that caught monsoon rain. Toward a grove of tamarisk trees, where the temple stood.

Not a grand temple. A hidden one.

Built from local stone and coral brick. A place not marked on any map, only named in vow:

Alaya Varahi. The Temple of the Primordial Flame.

She entered through the low threshold.

Inside, the air was cooler. Still. Thick with histories not spoken aloud. A set of steps led downward into a sanctum only lit by the open ceiling above; where the desert sun slanted in, dividing light from shadow in perfect symmetry.

There were three others waiting.

A Kushite initiate wearing a girdle of white shells.

A Greek priestess, her head shaved, her hands marked with blue ink.

And Neferka.

Older now, her braids wrapped in lapis cloth, her stance unshaken.

Vellichi nodded.

No words were exchanged. Only breath.

She stepped to the center of the chamber, where a shallow basin of red clay stood waiting. She knelt, unfastened the hem of her robe, and pulled the final scroll from its stitched lining.

The parchment trembled slightly in her hands, as if recognising its destination.

Etched in overlapping systems; Tamil siddham, Demotic glyphs, and star-mapped sigils, it was not a scroll of theology or trade. It was a convergence. A guide to sacred motion, breath, herbal correspondences, stellar alignments, and energy thresholds.

The priestess from Ionia began a chant. A sound that was not quite sung, more remembered.

Vellichi added her voice to it. The vibration filled the chamber. The serpent-lotus seal on her ring warmed, then flared with light.

They did not burn the scroll.

They buried it.

Wrapped in oiled linen and placed beneath the basin; sealed with salt, obsidian, and a single drop of each woman's blood. They covered it with sand from the altar floor, marking the spot with a triple spiral carved into the rim of the basin stone.

Then, they waited.

Hours later, the storm came, wild and unexpected. The sky turned copper. Wind screamed through the canyon like a warning. Sand poured through the temple's roof, burying the floor in minutes.

Vellichi stood still, the dust clinging to her lashes, arms open wide in invocation.

"This is not loss," she whispered in Tamil.

"This is remembrance sealed in earth."

And then—

Nothing but silence.

And the wind howling over what was no longer seen.

....

The Temple Uncovered, Red Sea Foothills, Midday Heat – Present Day

The desert wind had shifted sometime before dawn, leaving a fine crust of silt on the expedition tents. Selena stood beside a cluster of surveyors as the sun climbed higher, its white heat bouncing off rock and tarp. The dig site looked unremarkable at first; half-eroded, bone-dry stone walls buried beneath windblown sand. But the glyphs changed everything.

They had emerged only after a freak flash flood swept through the wadi days earlier, revealing the curvature of temple walls, inscriptions half-buried, but unmistakable, serpent entwined with lotus, coiled in a protective spiral. The very symbol that had haunted Selena's dreams since Rome.

The archaeological team was cautious. The site was undocumented, its foundation style pre-Ptolemaic, but the iconography hinted at syncretic rites; Tamil, Egyptian, even Hellenistic. One wall bore a carving of a woman standing in a flame halo, arms extended in dual gesture; protection and release. Another, a stylised map with sea routes running eastward, marked by stars.

Selena knelt, brushing sand from a line of glyphs still slick with moisture. Her breath caught. These weren't just devotional, they were directional. Coordinates encoded in prayer.

"He believed in empire by intellect."

Dr Layla's voice echoed in her mind, a conversation shared back in Alexandria.

"Alexander didn't come to Egypt just to rule it. He came to build something eternal. That's why he founded Alexandria; not just a city, but a portal. His legacy was not just conquest, but curation. Knowledge itself was his monument."

Selena could see it now. This temple tucked between land and sea, marked by fire and water, was not a site of worship alone. It was a sanctuary for transmission. The kind Alexander dreamed of preserving through scrolls, languages, emissaries.

And perhaps, it had never been lost; only waiting for the right current to lift the sand.

She turned toward the rising wind and felt something loosen inside her chest. Not a revelation.

A remembering.

The Letter, Guesthouse by the Red Sea – Dusk

The guesthouse was quiet, its sandstone walls warmed by the day's sun, now blushing rose under the fading light. The building itself was old; a converted Ottoman caravanserai perched just above the shoreline near Marsa Alam, its stone floors cooled by evening breezes and the low hum of ceiling fans. Jasmine vines crawled up one wall. A brass lantern flickered gently beside the writing desk.

Selena sat at the window with her journal open, the smell of salt and sandalwood clinging to her sleeves. Outside, the tide crept in slowly, a hush against the reef.

She dipped her pen in ink.

This letter wasn't to anyone she could name. Not Matteo. Not Layla. Not even Vellichi.

This was to the sea.

To time.

To memory itself.

"You were never silent.

You were waiting.

For someone who could listen with their bones.

I vow not to steal your stories.

I vow to carry them forward.

As flame.

As breath.

As dance."

A single wave broke loudly on the shore. She paused, letting the echo root itself in her ribs.

"This isn't research anymore.

It's return."

She placed the pen down gently.

Outside, the night had arrived quietly. The stars blinked like old eyes waking up.

And from the sea below, something answered.

Not in words.

But in warmth.

Like a vow accepted.

Reflections on the Lost Port

Selena stood on the ridge overlooking the excavation site just beyond the modern coast; a windswept plain of broken stone and salt-bitten silence. Beneath her feet lay the bones of Berenike, once a vital Red Sea port under Ptolemaic and Roman control, now crumbling into the sand like half-remembered scripture. Once, elephants bound for the imperial arenas of Rome were offloaded here. Once, Tamil spices, Nubian incense, and Persian textiles passed through the stone gates like offerings to time. Once, the sacred and the practical braided themselves into the rhythm of dockside ritual.

Even now, the remains of temple walls, votive niches, and storerooms clung to the landscape, whispering of their former purpose. Archaeologists had unearthed inscriptions in Tamil-Brahmi, Hellenic, and Demotic; unlikely siblings sharing the same breath. Clay amulets shaped like lotuses and serpents, shards of ritual vessels, fragments of star charts, all hinted that this had not merely been a trade station. It had been a threshold, a place of convergence between material exchange and spiritual transmission.

The air smelled of dust, salt, and iron; clean, sharp, ancient. Wind curled through the arches of partially revealed structures, playing melodies against stone like a forgotten reed instrument. In the distance, the Red Sea shimmered, unwavering, like a mirror held between worlds.

Selena closed her eyes, pressing her palm to the serpent-lotus seal now carved on a recovered altar slab.

"This was a sanctuary disguised as a port," she thought. "A school of fire-veiled knowledge, hidden in plain sight. They had not lost their wisdom to conquest. They had buried it, so one day, someone like me could find it again."

The temple was never built to be remembered in books.

It was built to be felt in the body.

And her body was finally listening.

A single tear slid down her cheek; not of grief, but recognition.

She wasn't just an archaeologist.

She was the answer the ruins had been waiting for.

Selena's Vow

Beneath the stars, beside the ancient sea, Selena whispered a vow; not to a god, not to a person, but to the land itself.

"I will carry what was meant to move.

I will speak what was once sealed.

I am not merely a seeker.

I am the return."

The wind didn't still.

It bowed.

Selena's circuit was now complete.

From root to crown, she no longer merely remembered.

She now embodied.

She turned from the ruins with the sun behind her. Not everything buried was lost. Some things were simply waiting to be spoken again.

The river never forgot.
It had only been waiting for her voice.

Selena's Diary Entry

Field Notes – Red Sea Guesthouse, Near Marsa Alam

Mission:

Investigate the convergence of Tamil-Chola emissaries with Egyptian temple culture at Berenike. Study seal iconography, trace sacred feminine transmission through trade ports, and identify symbolic language overlaps between Vedic and Hermetic systems.

Chakra Thread:

Root- Anchoring ancestral memory into the physical — the body as the first temple, the land as the ultimate scripture.

Crown- Connection to eternal memory — the cosmos as archive, where sacred knowledge circulates in stars, symbols, and sensation.

Keywords:

- Berenike Port
- Lotus-serpent glyph
- Port as sanctuary
- Fire-veiled rites
- Soul cartography
- Geo-memory
- "The temple was never meant to be known — only remembered"
- Scrolls sewn into silk hems
- Knowledge buried, not lostChapter Fourteen – The Dessert Remembers

Shiraz, Iran – Present Day

The descent into Shiraz came like slipping into an ancient poem. From the aircraft window, Selena watched as the Zagros Mountains unfurled beneath her like a braided spine; ridges rising in waves of rose gold and bone-white. The peaks cut sharp against the horizon, their crests dusted in snow despite the August heat. Valleys cupped pockets of olive groves, almond trees, and the ruins of forgotten caravanserais.

The Zagros range, she had read, had long been the cradle of Persia's sacred and economic pulse. Shepherds still moved along its terraced folds with rhythms older than the Silk Road. These mountains had once hidden Zoroastrian fire temples, hosted rebel philosophers, and guarded trade routes that ferried frankincense, silk, and sacred texts from east to west. They were not merely geographic, they were ancestral.

Selena pressed her palm against the window. She could feel the land reaching up like a memory.

But Shiraz had not been the original plan.

It began, unexpectedly, in Alexandria, three evenings earlier.

After a long research day at the Bibliotheca Alexandrina, Selena had been persuaded into dinner by Mira Hassan, Dr Layla's junior researcher. They'd walked together under lamps glowing amber along the Corniche before turning into the shadow of Trianon, a storied European-style café founded in the early 1900s.

The place still wore its Belle Époque bones: pressed tin ceilings, walnut counters, velvet drapes faded by sun and revolution. Rumour had it that Trianon had once hosted spies and poets during the British occupation. Now, it bore the hush of something between elegance and endurance.

Over plates of molokhia with garlic rice and grilled bream, Mira had passed Selena a folded page.

"Mehdi," she said, tapping the name scrawled on the back. "Shiraz. He knows the margins of the margins."

"What is this?" Selena asked, examining the sketch of a lotus-serpent sigil beside a fire altar.

Mira leaned in, voice dropping. "A memory preserved in exile. We found mention of it in a Persian-Tamil glossary that never made it to the public archives. Yazd. Zoroastrian. Maritime fringe. But it's not just a temple. It's a silence that held."

Selena had gone still.

Mira stirred her tea. "You asked me once if Alexandria remembered. So does the desert. But not through scrolls, through fire."

Now, sitting in the rear of a rattling taxi bound for Shiraz's old quarter, Selena clutched that note with the weight of something fated. Her backpack held the same essentials she carried since Guangzhou: field notes, voice recorder, and the onyx seal from Rome that still pulsed warm some days.

The streets of Shiraz unfurled like lines of a prayer. Cypress trees lined the boulevard leading to the Shah Cheragh Shrine, its blue-tiled minarets catching late sun like blades of sky. Market stalls brimmed with dried limes, saffron threads, figs, and Persian sweets layered in rosewater and pistachio.

Selena's driver gestured out the window: "Hafez. The tomb. You know?"

She nodded. She would visit. But first, she needed to find Mehdi.

Mira's words echoed again: It's not a site. It's a silence.

And she was ready to listen.

Yazd Desert – Zoroastrian Shrine, Late Afternoon

The memory of Mehdi's voice from the night before still sat with Selena as the sun lowered across the desert rim. They'd met in a quiet teahouse tucked behind Vakil Bazaar, candle-lit and perfumed with cardamom and rose. Mehdi had worn dark cotton robes and an amber bead around his wrist that he kept running through his fingers, as if decoding time.

"Silence is never empty in Yazd," he had said over black tea. "Especially not in the fire lands. The people there know how to guard a vow." He had handed her a folded slip of paper with a name: Parvaneh. "She'll be expecting you."

Now, hours later, Selena sat in the backseat of a pale green Peugeot 405, its upholstery cracked but clean, her small bag resting on her lap. The driver, Dariush, wore mirrored aviators and a gentle half-smile, humming softly to a song playing through the radio; an old ballad by Googoosh, crackling with static.

They had left Shiraz early that morning, heading north-northeast toward Yazd, the road cutting through vast, wind-scraped terrain. The Zagros Mountains faded behind them as ochre flats took their place, occasionally punctuated by the skeletal remnants of watchtowers or domed caravanserais that had once fed Silk Road travellers dates, goat's milk, and legends.

The landscape was stark but far from lifeless. Women moved in long robes between clustered homes with mud-brick walls and turquoise doorframes. Cypress trees marked old pilgrimage paths. Farmers squatted under low apricot trees, sorting almonds from their husks into woven baskets. Children chased after each other beside sun-bleached donkeys. Everything seemed slower, woven into the rhythm of dust and sun.

Around noon, they stopped at a roadside café outside Abarkuh, a one-story structure draped in flowering bougainvillaea. Inside, there were only three tables, a humming refrigerator, and the smell of something both spiced and sweet.

Selena was served a simple meal: ash-e reshteh (a thick herb and noodle soup), warm sangak bread, and small bowls of mast-o-khiar (yoghurt mixed with cucumber and mint). The owner, a woman in her sixties with silver bangles stacked up both arms, had nodded approvingly at Selena's Farsi attempt: "Kheyli mamnoon."

As they drove again, the road narrowed, climbing into the foothills of the desert plateau. At last, the sharp cliff face of Chak Chak appeared like a wound in the earth, flanked by rows of cypress and streaked by old mineral veins. Carved into the rock were ascending steps; jagged, uneven, leading up toward the famed Zoroastrian shrine.

Waiting at the base of the path stood a woman cloaked in deep indigo, a scarf tied around her hair in the old desert style. Her skin was copper-brown, lined gently at the eyes and mouth. Her presence held the stillness of stone, but her gaze sparkled with undeniable intelligence.

"You must be Selena," she said, her English soft and lilting. "I am Parvaneh. You've arrived on a good day. The wind is quiet."

She wore a long tunic ivory with saffron trim embroidered with flame motifs along the cuffs and collar, and around her neck hung a small pendant in the shape of a faravahar, the

Zoroastrian symbol of spirit and divine purpose. Her haie tucked beneath a delicately embroided shawl.

Selena bowed slightly, instinctively.

"I was told you might show me what still burns," she said.

Parvaneh smiled, then turned toward the cliff. "Come. The fire remembers."

And as Selena followed, her breath shallow with anticipation, she felt it again; that coiling awareness in her spine. The same heat she had felt in Alexandria and Rome. Whatever waited at the top of these stairs wasn't ancient. It was alive.

Inside the Shrine of Flame and the Murals, Yazd Mountains, Chak Chak – Early Evening

The cliffside breathed silence.

Selena stepped carefully over the stone threshold, her head bowed, not out of dogma, but deference. The entrance to the Chak Chak shrine was small, almost inconspicuous, as if the mountain itself had made a promise to keep this place veiled. She ducked slightly as she entered, the scent of sandalwood, copper, and dry firewood thickening the air with the weight of centuries.

Inside, the shrine was dim, womb-like. A natural spring trickled down one stone wall, the water glistening as if it carried memory. Brass vessels collected the sacred runoff in silence. No ornate domes. No grandeur. Just rock, fire, and silence, elemental honesty.

The flame at the heart of the shrine burned steadily in a bronze brazier, blue at its centre, rimmed in amber. It was said to have burned for over 2,500 years, tended by Zoroastrian guardians whose names had long faded into the dust. Selena stood still, her breath catching in her chest. There was no wind, no hum of machines, only the sound of her own pulse and the water's quiet song.

Parvaneh stood nearby, hands clasped, her eyes soft and unwavering. She didn't speak. She didn't need to. This was not a space for explanation; it was for recognition.

Selena turned, her eyes adjusting to the shifting firelight. And then she saw it.

On the stone wall behind the flame; half obscured by time and mineral staining, was a mural. Not vivid. Faint. A serpent coiled around a lotus, each scale inked in a now-faded crimson, the lotus blooming at the serpent's crown. The sigil from her dreams. From the scrolls. From the altar in Alexandria.

She felt her knees weaken.

Parvaneh noticed, gently guiding her to a low stone bench set against the wall. Selena lowered herself, hands trembling slightly, her fingers now unconsciously tracing the triadic pattern carved into the stone edge beneath her seat.

"Who painted this?" she whispered.

Parvaneh sat beside her. "No one knows exactly. Some believe the mural was added by refugees; travelers who carried stories from the east. We know that in the 11th century, during times of persecution and upheaval, monks and mystics from many lands passed through Yazd. Tamil. Sufi. Persian. Some stayed. Some disappeared."

Selena's throat was dry. She reached for her water bottle and sipped, the metal cool against her lips. The fire crackled once, as if exhaling.

"The flame," she said, her voice hoarse. "Is it always this... blue?"

Parvaneh smiled faintly. "Only when it listens."

For a long moment, neither of them spoke.

Then, slowly, Selena stood and stepped forward. She knelt before the flame, palms open on her thighs. No prayer formed. But something older stirred. Her body knew how to be still. How to hold memory in silence.

The mural behind her seemed to breathe with the flickering light.

And in that stillness, in that sacred hush, the fire within her stirred.

A current moved up her spine, not forcefully, but like a rising tide meeting a familiar shore.

The air thickened, time folded.

The flame whispered in ancient tongue, not of words but feeling.

The mountain did not conceal. It protected.

The fire did not burn. It remembered.

Selena exhaled softly, and as her eyes fluttered closed, the echo of another fire flickered in her mind; distant, desert-bound, hidden behind veils of time.

Her breath slowed. The shrine dimmed. And the memory opened like a door.

....

Dream Trace – Zahara's Final Crossing, Persian Gulf Coast, Circa 12th Century CE

The wind off the gulf tasted of copper and coming rain.

Zahara stood beneath the shadow of a sun-bleached arch, her cloak drawn tight against her shoulders, a satchel of scrolls pressed close to her ribs. The air smelled of salt, smoke, and saffron oil; the markers of a bustling port now emptied under threat. Behind her, the city's sandstone alleys lay hushed, veiled in the hush before a storm. Before exile.

She had not always been Zahara.

And somehow, within the logic of the dream, Selena knew this. She could feel the shift. The soul had turned a corner. The name Vellichi had been sung once in temples; now it echoed differently in Zahara's bones. A new name, same flame. Same vow.

Zahara's face was veiled, but her eyes were fierce, lined with kohl and wind. The hem of her indigo robe was stained from river dust and ritual ash; traces of the sanctuary she had just left behind. A monastery carved into the cliffs, half temple, half refuge. There, she and the others had preserved what they could: scrolls written in a hybrid tongue of Tamil, Persian, and star-mapped glyphs. Cosmologies etched in ink made of lapis and clove, folded tightly into flameproof silks.

The wind carried voices now; faint, hurried.

She turned. A boy, no more than sixteen, barefoot, breathless, came running up the path.

Behind her, a flicker caught her eye, on the wall of the passage leading back into the cave. A palm print, darkened with age, larger than hers. Zahara stepped toward it and lifted her hand, aligning it without touch. It pulsed faintly, as though it knew her. Not a relic. A reminder. Someone had come before her, or after.

"They're coming. From the north. Ships on the horizon."

Zahara didn't flinch. She simply nodded.

"Then it's time."

She pressed a pouch into the boy's hands. "Take this east. Find the firekeepers. Don't open it. Don't stop."

He looked at her, eyes wide with the weight of the trust.

Then he ran.

Behind her, the last remaining monk stepped from the threshold of the cave sanctuary; white-bearded, his robes greyed with age and devotion.

"You'll go west?" he asked, his voice like parchment cracking.

Zahara nodded. "The coast holds one last gate. There's a temple carved into the rock, where the lotus-serpent was once invoked. I'll leave the final scroll there."

"If the storm reaches you first—"

"It won't."

She met his eyes. No fear. Just certainty born of lifetimes.

Then she turned, heading down the cliffside trail that wound toward the surf like a braid unraveling. The sea was growing restless, wind scraping whitecaps across the bay, clouds churning overhead.

When she reached the cove, the sand stung her skin like whispered warnings.

The temple was no more than a cavity in the rock, weathered and sacred. Inside, a carved altar, a scorched bowl, and above it, the lotus-serpent etched in perfect spirals, still intact.

Zahara bowed. Unwrapped the scroll. Placed it within a clay vessel.

Sealed it with wax. And buried it beneath the altar stone.

As Zahara placed the scroll into the hollow carved beneath the altar, a current moved through Selena; not a memory, but a cellular knowing. This wasn't Vellichi's story any longer. This was a life born of exile, of fire-wrapped silence. Zahara. She

179

whispered the name inwardly, a syllable that pulsed behind her ribs. Not a disguise, but a continuation. A rebirth. She was no longer the one who carried the flame. She had become its keeper.

Above her, thunder rolled like a drumbeat of memory.

She rose, stepped outside.

The first drops fell.

And in the moment before lightning struck, the wind carried something unexpected; a song, from the shoreline below. A woman's voice, weaving syllables into the wind.

She turned. A boat. A hooded figure at the helm.

Recognition bloomed; not as name, but as presence.

The soul twin. The storm broke. The vision scattered like leaves in wind.

....

Selena awoke with tears on her cheeks. Her fingers curled around the edge of the stone bench at Chak Chak, her breath short, her pulse wild.

Not Vellichi. Zahara.

The line had continued. The vow had not ended. Only changed form.

She sat motionless as the shrine returned to silence, only the fire still speaking.

Yazd Shrine Courtyard, Twilight

The desert held its breath.

Selena sat on a low stone bench in the courtyard just outside the fire shrine, her shawl wrapped loosely over her shoulders. The air had shifted; the day's heat now softened into lavender wind, the sand around her bathed in mauve and gold. Palm shadows stretched across the walls. From somewhere behind the shrine, a goat bleated once, then silence returned, thick and knowing.

She hadn't spoken since waking from the dream.

Zahara.

The name rang in her chest like a bell struck deep. It wasn't just a memory; it was a handprint on the inside of her skin.

Not Vellichi. Not anymore.

The dream hadn't shattered her. It had reconfigured her. The moment Zahara had turned into the wind, scroll tucked into her robes and exile behind her eyes, Selena had known. This wasn't about returning to power. It was about protecting what power feared.

She glanced down at her palm. Her fingers still tingled from where she had traced the lotus-serpent on the mural earlier, the sigil now etched not just in pigment, but in presence. She could still see the way it had wrapped around the fire altar. A language with no alphabet. A vow with no sound.

She sat unmoving, letting the warmth of the fire and the cold of memory meet in her body. The shrine wasn't just a space; it was an echo chamber. An Akashic node. A living archive encoded in silence. Every chant whispered in exile, every vow sealed with ash and intention; it lingered here in vibration. Not stored in scrolls, but in frequency. And now, it vibrated inside her.

Just then, Mehdi stepped into view, emerging from the corridor like someone cautious not to disturb a prayer.

"You're alright?" he asked gently.

Selena nodded. "More than alright. It's like... something remembered me."

He didn't press further. Only offered a slow, respectful smile, and a thermos of hot rose tea he had brought from the car.

She accepted it with both hands, grateful.

In the distance, the last light of the sun dipped behind the cragged Zagros Mountains, gilding their ridges in amber. Selena inhaled the scent of rose petals, fire smoke, and cooling stone. Her journal lay open on her lap, a few lines already scratched in half-thought. But words felt too small right now.

The silence around her wasn't empty.

It was a container.

And within it, her vow lived. Above her, thunder rolled like a drumbeat of memory.

She rose, stepped outside.

The first drops fell.

And in the moment before lightning struck, the wind carried something unexpected; a song, from the shoreline below. A woman's voice, weaving syllables into the wind.

She turned. A boat. A hooded figure at the helm.

Recognition bloomed; not as name, but as presence.

The soul twin. The storm broke. The vision scattered like leaves in wind.

As she gazed at the horizon beyond Yazd, Selena thought of the sea again; the invisible thread binding deserts to coasts, shrines to ports. Empire always travelled on water.

The Cholas had known it; their ships once mapped the monsoons as faithfully as priests mapped the stars. The Persians understood it too, their fire altars guiding sailors through night winds long before compass needles pointed north. Even the

British, centuries later, had merely sailed the same old tide beneath a different flag.

The instruments changed; sails, cannons, steam, but the impulse was the same. To master the sea was to master story.

And somewhere within her, she could feel the tide turning back, not toward conquest, but remembrance.

The flame hadn't died.
It had only been waiting for her return.

Selena's Diary Entry

Field Notes – Shiraz to Yazd (Chak Chak Shrine), Iran

Mission:

Trace the Zoroastrian–Tamil transmission: verify the lotus–serpent sigil in Yazd; locate records or oral memory of firekeeper routes, cliff monasteries, and coastal cache sites tied to Zahara's deposit. Prioritise: (1) shrine oral histories (Parvaneh/Mehdi networks), (2) coastal temple candidates along Persian Gulf, (3) hybrid-script fragments (Tamil–Persian–stellar).

Chakra Thread:

Root: desert ground, mountain-threshold steadiness.

Sacral: fire-current rising at the brazier; vow-as-creation.

Solar Plexus: purpose clarified (keeper, not courier).

Heart: ache/recognition at soul twin on the water.

Third Eye: clear vision of Zahara and the cache; symbol recall.

Crown: initiation-by-flame; silence as temple.

Selena's Reflection:

Not Vellichi this time. Zahara. The lineage didn't end; it changed function — from carrier to keeper. The shrine isn't a relic; it's a living archive where vows are stored as **frequency**, not text. The blue in the fire felt like consent. I'm not researching memory; I'm re-entering it.

Repeated Phrase:

"The fire remembers."

"Silence is a container, not an absence."

Keywords:

- Akashic Echoes

- Zahara (Rebirth Identity)
- Sacred exile / chosen silence
- Zoroastrian flame rites
- Chak Chak shrine
- Sound as scripture
- Monastery as memory vault
- Serpent-lotus sigil
- Mehdi / Parvaneh
- Sufi veils / Persian scroll-work
- Guardian of the Flame
- Silence as protection, not absence

Chapter Fifteen –
The Shores of
Silence

Historical Echo – From Persia to the Swahili Coast – Present Day

The line from Yazd to Lamu wasn't a flight path. It was a tide line.

Two things pulled Selena east-south from the fire temple. First, the Zahara vision had fixed a final cache on a coast where languages braided, Tamil, Persian, Arabic, Swahili; "a rock-temple facing monsoon winds," guarded not by walls but by chants. Second, Parvaneh's quiet aside in the shrine corridor: *When the firekeepers fled, some followed the incense winds by dhow—down Oman, past Hormuz, across to the Swahili isles. The vows didn't drown. They sang.*

Maps and margins backed the hunch. Mehdi's notes traced frankincense routes that curved from Hormuz to the Lamu archipelago, and a Persian–Tamil glossary scrap Mira had shared in Alexandria mentioned "sea-songs" kept by "women of the coral towns." If the scrolls were ever broken, the code would persist as rhythm.

So Selena chose Lamu, an island that had traded in silence and sound for a thousand years. She wasn't chasing an artifact anymore. She was following a living repository: breath, drum, vow. From fire to water, from keeper to choir, the work was the same. Listen for the place that still remembers. And let it teach you how.

Selena's journey from Persia to Kenya felt like slipping between two elemental realms, from fire to water.

She had departed from Tehran in the early morning haze, after one final visit to the Yazd fire temple. Her satchel still smelled faintly of ash and rosewater. Onboard the flight to Nairobi, she watched the Iranian plateau disappear below in soft pinks and terracotta ridges, the desert giving way to clouds like pulled wool.

In Nairobi, the air changed; it was heavier, warmer, infused with rain-washed soil and the faint perfume of jacaranda blossoms. There was a weight of memory in the humidity, as if the land itself sweat history.

From there, she took a regional flight toward the Kenyan coast, the ocean unrolling beneath her like a silk map. When the plane descended over the Lamu archipelago, the islands looked scattered and delicate, like remnants of an ancient calligraphy brush dipped in seafoam.

Her arrival at Manda Airport was quiet. A small, sun-baked airstrip. No chaos. Just sandals scraping stone, seagulls wheeling low, and a lone sign pointing toward the ferry dock. There, she boarded a weathered wooden dhow-style ferry heading for Lamu Old Town.

She found a seat on the lower deck, shaded from the sun but open to the breeze. Salt air clung to her skin, and somewhere distant, the call to prayer mingled with birdsong and the clinking of shells hung along nearby jetties. The ferry was slow, not in delay, but in tempo. A reminder that memory didn't move fast here. It rippled.

She glanced around, and by chance, or something more, found herself seated beside a man in his late fifties, with skin the colour of sea-aged teak and a calm gaze behind wire-rimmed glasses. He wore a loose cotton tunic and carried a canvas bag crammed with books.

"First time to Lamu?" he asked in a gentle baritone.

Selena nodded. "I'm following... tides. And echoes."

That made him smile.

He introduced himself as Professor Elijah Mutua, from the University of Nairobi; a maritime historian with a specialisation in Indian Ocean trade networks. He had been returning from a research visit to Kipini, studying inscriptions left on mosque walls by medieval sailors.

Over the gentle lapping of waves and the rhythmic creak of wood, their conversation began with shared curiosity and soon unraveled into a rich tapestry of forgotten routes, hybrid rites, and cultural residues. He spoke of Swahili-Tamil exchanges with casual reverence, as if discussing an old family secret.

"Most people think the Indian influence in Kenya began with colonial indenture," he said, gesturing to the horizon. "But centuries before the British drew their maps, Tamil ships were already docking here."

He went on to explain that Chola fleets had reached the East African coast by the 11th century. Not as conquerors, but as sacred traders. They brought textiles, beads, bronze, and music. They left behind temple fragments, oral chants, ritual gestures, and bloodlines.

"The Swahili coast didn't forget," he said. "It absorbed."

He spoke of a specific coral temple, now lost beneath the tide, where inscriptions in early Tamil script were once photographed; a story Selena would revisit later over a visit to University of Nairobi to chat to Professor Elijah Mutua, when their paths crossed again during her archival visit in Nairobi.

For now, she simply listened.

The ferry passed beneath a sky turning soft with dusk, and she felt it again; the familiar hum at her spine. Not quite memory. Not quite vision.

But the unmistakable rhythm of return.

Lamu Old Town – Morning Walk

Selena wandered through the old town's labyrinthine streets, the coral stone beneath her feet was warm and uneven. The town moved slowly, like a prayer mid-breath. Women in layered kangas walked in pairs, their laughter hidden behind patterned veils. Donkeys clopped past with baskets of green mangoes and sweet potatoes. The smell of cardamom, tamarind, and drying fish drifted between carved wooden doors.

Children played with marbles near an old mosque, their voices blending into the distant rhythm of a taarab melody playing from an unseen radio.

She paused at a centuries-old baobab tree, its trunk twisted and vast, like a memory holding its breath. A local elder sat nearby on a stone bench, fingers stroking prayer beads.

"You're not lost," he said, looking up with a knowing smile. "The island calls who it remembers."

Selena smiled. "And if I've never been here?"

"Not in this skin," he replied, tapping his chest, "but your steps are old."

The Chants - Manda Island, Kenya

The chant rose slowly, not from any amplified speaker or temple bell, but from a circle of seated elders under the twisted boughs of a baobab tree. It was dusk, and the sky over Manda Island shimmered like silk stretched across fire. The ocean lapped gently at the shore, an eternal witness.

Selena stood at the edge of the gathering, barefoot in the coral-sand soil. Her breath slowed. The sound; deep, rhythmic, resonant, echoed something she had only previously encountered in dream. She didn't know the words, but she recognised their structure. The cadence matched the devotional syllables she had traced in copper-scroll fragments from the Tamil coast. A rhythm not meant to entertain, but to invoke.

She glanced at the woman beside her; Asha, one of the keepers of oral histories in the Lamu Archipelago. Her face, lined and luminous, tilted upward toward the canopy. The chant continued, interwoven with drumbeats, soft, syncopated, sacred.

Selena's skin tingled.

These were no ordinary songs.

They were codes; ancestral algorithms spoken in tongues that carried across oceans and centuries. Some verses were clearly Swahili, but layered beneath them were harmonics and half-tones reminiscent of Tamil and Sanskrit intonations. And suddenly, she saw it, not as a coincidence, but as a legacy.

The Chola presence here hadn't vanished. It had transformed.

Centuries earlier, the Chola Empire had reached far beyond the Indian subcontinent; not just through warships and emissaries, but through artisans, traders, and temple dancers. Their fleets had sailed past Oman and Hormuz, stopping at Red Sea ports before curving south along the African coast. Manda and Lamu, positioned along this maritime axis, were known contact points. Temple foundations, Tamil-Brahmi inscriptions, and gold-threaded textiles unearthed in fragments now seemed less like anomalies and more like signposts.

Even now, the fingerprints of that connection remained visible across Kenya's cultural canvas. Indian settlements in Mombasa, Nairobi, and Lamu had roots that stretched back well before British colonial routes. Gujarati, Tamil, and Malayali families formed trading guilds and spiritual communities, building temples and introducing foods like dosa, chapati, and lentil stews that became part of Swahili cuisine. Mango pickles, sandalwood, jasmine oil. Sarees and kangas sharing patterns. Even the architecture, stucco arches, inner courtyards, latticed balconies, all revealed an architectural osmosis.

The Chola Empire had not merely touched this shore. It had seeded something.

And it was in these chants, Selena realised, that memory survived; not just in bricks or scrolls, but in breath.

She pressed a hand to her heart, the rhythm of the drum syncing with her own pulse. Around her, the elders continued the invocation, their eyes closed, their spines straight. This was not performance. It was prayer as transmission.

One of the elders opened her eyes and looked directly at Selena. There was no surprise in her gaze, only recognition.

As if she'd been expected.

Dream Trace – Zahara on the Swahili Coast, Circa 12th Century CE

The scent of tamarind and turmeric floated on the air, thick with salt and smoke. Zahara stood beneath a canopy of coral-stone arches, her bare feet resting on woven reed mats. Around her, the coastal breeze carried the murmur of tides and the clatter of market life; spices being weighed, ivory being loaded into carved dhows, gold glinting in the sun like scattered vows.

But Zahara wasn't here to trade.

She was here to hide something holy.

The settlement rose in tiers of stone and carved wood, blending Persian, Arab, and Indian aesthetics into a uniquely Swahili rhythm. White-plastered walls reflected the glare of the sun, while shutters bore intricate floral latticework. Beneath it all ran narrow alleys like arteries, pulsing with the hum of languages: Tamil, Swahili, Arabic, Old Persian. Not a melting pot but a meeting point.

She had arrived weeks earlier under cover of a merchant caravan, posing as a trader of frankincense and saffron oil. In truth, she carried the last of the scrolls; cosmologies inked in lapis and soot, folded within a seal-wrapped linen pouch. Texts that survived fire, flight, and betrayal. Texts now destined for hiding once more.

Zahara adjusted the amber pendant at her throat, a protective talisman carved with a wave-script sigil, gifted to her in Persia before her escape. Its warmth pulsed faintly now, responding to something. Or someone.

As she approached the shrine, hidden in a grove behind a spice orchard, voices rose in song. Not Swahili. Not Tamil. But both.

A group of women stood in a circle, swaying gently as they chanted. Young and old. Heads wrapped in dyed cottons and silks. Their rhythm was precise, ancient. Their mudras traced spirals in the air. Zahara's heart clenched. This wasn't imitation. It was inheritance. Somehow, the rites had survived, carried by dancers, weavers, mothers. Transformed, but intact.

She felt her past lives bloom behind her eyes. Not as stories. As remembering.

One of the women turned and met Zahara's gaze. A scar shaped like a crescent moon curved beneath her left eye.

"You carry fire," the woman said in Tamil-accented Swahili. "But not all flames are meant to burn. Some are meant to seed."

Zahara knelt, removed the scroll pouch from under her robe, and placed it in a clay urn beneath a sacred fig tree. She whispered a vow, not of secrecy, but of song.

If the scrolls were ever destroyed, the words would live in chant.

Thunder rolled in the distance. The tide surged. And with it came a presence.

From the tree line, a lone figure stepped forward; male, cloaked in indigo, face veiled against the dust. But his energy was unmistakable.

The soul twin.

He nodded once, then held out a hand, not in invitation, but in witnessing.

She bowed her head. There would be no escape this time. Only continuation.

As Zahara rose, the chants grew louder, folding around her, like silk and sky. The wind lifted her veil. The pendant at her throat glowed briefly, then dimmed. A single drop of rain struck the earth.

The cycle had closed.

But the story was not finished.

....

Coastal Guesthouse, Lamu Island, Dusk

Selena awoke with salt on her lips.

Not sweat. Not sea spray. But something subtler, the taste of remembrance.

She sat upright on the low wooden bed, mosquito net falling like sheer gauze around her. The ceiling fan turned lazily overhead. Outside the open windows, the air was thick with the scent of hibiscus and charcoal fires. Somewhere nearby, a child was laughing. A dhow horn echoed across the water.

For a moment, she didn't move.

Her breath came slow, uneven. The dream hadn't faded. It lingered in her skin. Zahara's voice. The chants. The pendant pulsing at her throat. The soul twin's eyes like a memory made flesh.

Selena rose, feet bare on the cool terracotta tiles, and stepped out onto the guesthouse's wraparound veranda. The wooden slats creaked underfoot. From here, she had a clear view of the Lamu channel; dhows slicing the coppery water, sails curved like calligraphy.

The sky was pink and vermilion, melting into the sea. Swahili call to prayer drifted on the breeze, blending with the rhythm of drums from deeper inland. The island moved at the pace of tides and memory.

The guesthouse itself was a preserved coral-stone merchant home, a relic from the 19th century now repurposed into a retreat for scholars and travelers. Worn lanterns hung from carved eaves. Bougainvillea vines crawled over the stucco walls. Inside, the scent of sandalwood mingled with coastal air and clove tea steeping in the lounge.

Selena leaned against the wooden balustrade, hands still tingling.

In her palm, she clutched the amber pendant she had worn since Oman; dormant for days, but now warm again, as if awakened by the dream. No... not just the dream. The memory.

It was Zahara now. Not Vellichi.

The flame had crossed oceans. So had she.

Selena exhaled. The sea answered.

She could still feel the clay urn beneath the fig tree, the way the scroll fit perfectly inside it. The chants weren't symbolic. They were repositories, breathing the memory forward. She had been part of that transmission. And she was again.

From her canvas satchel, she pulled out her leather journal and flipped to a fresh page. Her fingers moved slowly, tracing a spiral before writing, in a hand that didn't feel entirely hers:

"The vow didn't end in exile. It transformed into rhythm."

She paused, pen hovering, before continuing:

"And the soul didn't forget. It sang."

Behind her, the room darkened. But the sea and the flame within her, stayed lit.

The song remembered what her silence had buried.

Selena's Diary Entry

Field Notes – Lamu Island, Kenya
Mission

To follow the echoes of the chants — not only through texts and murals, but through living voices. Lamu wasn't just a point on the map. It was a vessel. The memory was not buried here. It was sung. And I had to remember how to listen. Zahara didn't survive by speaking — she endured by transmitting. Through gesture, rhythm, and vow. I now understand the silence was never empty. It was calibrated.

Chakra Thread

Solar Plexus: Power reclaimed through voice and memory. The chant was not about sound — it was about recognition. In reclaiming the solar plexus, I'm reclaiming my agency, my purpose, my lineage. I speak not for others, but from the truth that outlived conquest, exile, and erasure.

Selena's Reflection:

The silence here doesn't demand stillness — it sings.

Each chant I hear is an archive, every breath a script older than ink.

Zahara's vow didn't perish with the temple fires. It crossed oceans disguised as melody.

The Chola emissaries didn't vanish; they became vibration — carried by mothers, merchants, and midwives who turned survival into song.

When I stood among the chanters, I felt the desert's flame become tide.

The vow has changed form again, and this time, it is **voice**.

Repeated Phrase:

"The vow became rhythm."

"The sea remembers the fire."
Keywords:

- Zahara
- Amber pendant reactivation
- Dhow
- Lamu
- Spiral
- Scroll
- Tuning
- Soul Twin
- Chola trade routes to East Africa
- Baobab circle / ancestral chant / drum prayer
- Exile as transmission
- Professor Elijah Mutua
- Rememberance as rhythm

Chapter Sixteen –
The Map That
Breathes

Lamu Island – Present Day

The air had thickened. Not with heat, but with knowing.

Selena sat cross-legged on the rooftop of her guesthouse, the adhan echoing faintly in the distance. Below, the winding alleyways of Lamu were slowing for the night: fishermen hauling in the last of the day's catch, children kicking a frayed ball under the palm trees, voices low in Swahili and Gujarati. The scent of woodsmoke, cardamom, and sea drifted up with the breeze.

She had not left the island since arriving.

And yet, she had never traveled further.

It began that morning, during a sunrise meditation by the mangroves. She had chanted the mantras softly, as Zeinab had taught her in Alexandria, letting the syllables rise from root to crown. But this time, something cracked. Not in her, in everything. She had seen it in a single flash; the submerged ruins of Muziris, the obsidian caves near Oman, the chanting wells of Tamil Nadu, the altar stones in Kom Ombo, the shrine at Chak Chak, the hidden cove on the Swahili coast, the mosaic dancer in Rome, all glowing. Connected. Alive.

Not ruins. Nerve endings.

She had stumbled back to her room, hands shaking, and opened her journal. But it wasn't the journal that held the map. It was her. She dropped to her knees, lit a single flame, and inhaled deeply.

Then, without prompt or resistance, she slipped inward.

....

The Remembering of Light – The Soul Map Revealed

She wasn't walking; she was moving through all of them at once.

Kom Ombo. Yazd. Muziris. Alexandria. Lamu. Rome. The Red Sea. The Gulf. The silk-lined pages and fire-lit temples.

Mayilai, chanting beside ocean wells, her voice laced with salt and saffron smoke.

Vellichi, holding a copper scroll beneath desert stars.

Zahara, sealing a fire-writ vow in stone.

Selena, wrapped in their memory and spiralling inward.

At the center, beneath a sky not bound by stars but by memory, stood a figure.

Still. Waiting.

The Soul Twin.

He was exactly as she remembered, and not at all. Ageless. Familiar. The shape of him woven into her silence long before any name had been spoken. His eyes shimmered with aeons, oceans of recognition.

This time, he spoke.

"We are not bound by time. But we are shaped by it." Selena stepped closer. Her breath caught.

"You're real," she whispered. "You've been following me."

"No," he said gently. "We've been orbiting each other, across lifetimes. Not seeking... remembering."

He held out his hand. In his palm was a map; not parchment, not paper but living light, lines glowing in ink and rhythm. She reached for it, but paused.

"What are we?" she asked.

His gaze deepened.

"Soul twins. Not lovers in the human sense. Not destined to complete each other but to mirror."

"Why?"

"Because you hold a thread of the flame, and so do I. Each time we meet, we bring the fire back into balance. We awaken the parts the other forgot."

"Your knowing completes my vow. My silence steadies your sight."

Selena blinked. A tear slipped sideways, suspended in the dreamscape air.

"Why do we forget?" she asked.

He smiled softly. "Because forgetting is part of the journey. Re-remembering is how we rewrite the vow."

"What vow?"

He stepped closer. Between them, the map pulsed like breath.

"To carry the sacred. To protect what cannot be written. To remember through the body what history will try to erase."

For a moment, she felt herself expand beyond form, as if she were all three at once: Mayilai, Vellichi, Zahara, and Selena. And across from her stood the constant: the one who returned each time she was close to forgetting.

"You waited for me," she whispered.

"Always," he said. "And I'll wait again if I must. But not in longing. In purpose."

He pressed the glowing map into her hands.

"You are not the seeker," he said, voice tender as wind.

"You are the remembered. The one who never broke the thread."

The dreamspace began to dissolve like smoke unraveling, like tide leaving shell. His form shimmered, then began to fade.

"Will I see you again?"

His final words came as light:

"In every vow you honour. In every silence you carry with courage. That's where I live."

The light folded. The breath left her body.

....

Professor Elijah Mutua – Archives in the Sand, Lamu Fort, Midday – Present Day

The sun hung high over Lamu Town, casting long shadows across the coral-stone ramparts of Lamu Fort. Built by the Omanis, shaped by the Swahili, and weathered by centuries, the fort now served as a museum and cultural archive, an unlikely yet perfect place to house stories too resilient to die.

Selena had arranged to meet Professor Elijah Mutua in the inner courtyard, just beside a weatherworn dhow sail strung like a tapestry over old cannon mounts. When he arrived, she recognised him instantly; same bone-white linen shirt, same thoughtful gaze that had lingered on waves during their ferry ride from Manda.

"Still charting maps of memory, I see," he said by way of greeting, gesturing to the leather-bound notebook in her lap.

Selena smiled. "Always. You mentioned something on the boat, about an undocumented Indian presence on this coast, centuries before colonial records?"

He nodded, lowering himself onto the bench beside her. "Yes. And you were right to ask about the Cholas."

He pulled out a laminated chart from his canvas tote bag; a reproduction of an ancient maritime route, annotated with his notes in red ink.

"The Cholas weren't just warriors. They were navigators, patrons of cosmology, temple builders, traders of perfumes, gemstones, even sacred texts. Manda Bay and Lamu were part of a larger Chola trade arc that extended from Southern India to Berenike, Hormuz, and the Swahili coast."

Selena leaned in. "There's an oral chant I heard here... Swahili in rhythm, but the intonation felt Tamil. Almost Vedic."

Elijah's eyes lit up. "Yes. That's been part of our oral ethnomusicology research for years. The older women of Pate and Siyu speak of 'singing the sun across the sea.' There are tonal signatures in their lullabies that mirror ragas used in South Indian devotional music."

He paused, then handed her a thin booklet of field notes and chant transcriptions.

"One of our team found this in a chest of family heirlooms in Shela village. It mentions a woman arriving with scrolls... during the great tides. Some believe she was a goddess. Others, a merchant. A guardian."

Selena's throat tightened.

Zahara.

"This woman, does she have a name in the oral record?"

Elijah flipped a page, finger landing on a phrase written in Swahili script.

"Binti wa Mwanga wa Bahari."

Daughter of the Ocean Light.

"She was believed to have come from the east, carrying stories that could not be spoken aloud. They say she buried her songs in the sand."

Selena closed her notebook, fingers pressing into the cover like sealing a page in her chest.

"She didn't bury them," she said softly. "She encoded them."

They sat in silence for a moment, the wind rustling the old sail above them. The fort around them, once a stronghold of empire, now sheltered archives built not of dominion but memory.

Elijah stood and extended a hand.

"If you ever decide to return, we're creating a permanent exhibition. 'Echoes of the Tide: India and Africa's Lost Maritime Legacies.' I'd like you to help curate it."

Selena rose, grasping his hand, her voice steady. "Yes. I'd like that very much."

Rooftop at Dawn – The Map Lives Within, Lamu Island – Present Day

Just before sunrise, Selena woke with the map still glowing behind her eyelids.

She wasn't in a trance anymore, she was fully awake, fully here. But the dream had not ended. It had simply shifted dimensions. The sounds of Lamu filtered in slowly; the distant bleat of a goat, the flutter of linen curtains, the call to prayer echoing like a river of vowels through coral-stone alleyways.

She sat upright on the rooftop terrace of the guesthouse, wrapped in a wool shawl, her body still warm from the imprint of the dream. The sea beyond shimmered in pearl-grey silence.

A small brass lamp with a glass cover still flickered near her, left burning from the night before. The journal lay open on her lap, the edges ruffled by salt wind. On the last page, drawn not with conscious thought but from something deeper, was a sketch, the same triadic spiral. The soul map.

But now, it wasn't just a symbol. It was a route.

Each arc represented a port. A scroll. A vow.

- Mayiladuthurai, Tamil Nadu, India: The awakening.
- Muziris, Kerala, India: The first crossing.
- Kanchipuram, Tamil Nadu, India: The lineage.
- Colombo, Sri Lanka: The betrayal.
- Malacca, Malaysia: The divergence.
- Guangzhou, China: The veil.
- Oman, Middle East: The threshold.
- Petra, Jordan: The guardian.
- Alexandria, Egypt: The summons.
- Kom Ombo, Egypt: The rite.
- Rome, Italy: The mirror.
- Shiraz, Iran: The silence.
- Yazd, Iran: The flame.
- Lamu, Kenya, Africa: The voice and The map made whole.

All fourteen formed the spiral. The soul thread. Her map.

She unwrapped the silk pendant she had carried since Oman. It had never felt like the right time to open it, until now.

Inside, folded so precisely it looked like breath held in cloth, was a fragment of parchment, older than any in her collection. The ink had faded to near invisibility, but the texture was unmistakable. Palm-fiber papyrus. Tamil-Brahmi strokes. Beneath it; the faint outline of a wave-shaped glyph, not just drawn, but burned gently into the fibers.

The scroll had travelled through fire. And survived.

So had she.

Selena looked up. The dawn cracked open along the sea's edge, casting coral and gold across the rooftops. Somewhere below, fishermen stirred their nets. A boy pedaled past on a bicycle, balancing trays of samosas and cardamom buns on his head.

The island was waking.

So was she.

Selena's Vow – Lamu Shoreline, Sunset

The tide had gone out, leaving ripples in the sand like an ancient script only water could write.

Selena walked barefoot along the edge, the hem of her dress brushing against her ankles, still damp from the sea. She carried no journal, no scroll, no voice recorder. Only a single palm-leaf bundle, now wrapped in red cloth; the final page she had unwrapped that morning.

The pendant. The wave-inscribed glyph. The fire-etched parchment.

She knelt where the sand met coral rock, wind curling her hair around her face like a veil. No tourists wandered nearby.

Just the horizon, stretching wide and warm, and the dusky shapes of wooden dhows bobbing like old memories offshore.

She buried the scroll at the base of a salt-blanched tree. Not to lose it but to root it.

She whispered something then. Not in English. Not in Tamil. Not even in Zahara's language.

But in the breath-between-languages.

A vow. A return. Not to power. To presence.

To speak again, as the women before her had spoken in stone, in smoke, in silence, and in sound.

When she rose, she did not look back.

The map was no longer something she followed.

It was something she had become.

She hadn't been tracing history,
She had been remembering herself.

Selena's Diary Entry

Field Notes – Lamu Island, Kenya

Mission:

To integrate — not research, but embodiment.

To understand that the soul's pilgrimage was never about proof, but remembrance.

To hold within me the living map that threads fire to water, vow to voice, silence to sound.

To live the continuation, not merely document it.

Chakra Thread:

Heart: Unification of all echoes — compassion as the centre of memory.

Throat: Expression without language — truth through resonance, chant, and breath.

Third Eye: Vision beyond lifetimes — the capacity to see what the soul remembers.

Crown: Illumination — realisation that the seeker and the sacred were never separate.

Selena's Reflection:

I am not tracing the past anymore — I am walking within its pulse.

Every vow uttered in silence now hums beneath my skin.

The map is not something to follow; it's something I've become.

The Soul Twin was right: forgetting is part of remembering.

It's how the vow renews itself — through each life, each breath, each act of courage.

The sea, the flame, the voice — all speak one language: *continuity.*

And I carry it now.

Not as burden.

As song.

Repeated Phrase:

"You are the remembered."

"The map lives within."

"The vow does not end — it breathes."

Keywords:

- Integration / Soul Twin / Map of Light
- Fire–Water Union / Embodied Continuity
- Professor Elijah Mutua / Chola–Swahili Legacy
- Heart–Throat–Crown alignment
- Vow as vibration / Completion of the cycle
- Remembrance as destiny / Light as cartography

Chapter Seventeen – Where the River Bends

Thanjavur, Tamil Nadu, India – Present Day

Selena had crossed seas before, but this return felt different. From the moment her flight left the tarmac in Lamu, a hum had begun beneath her ribs; an invisible thread drawing her eastward, not to discover, but to remember.

She flew into Trichy International Airport just after dawn. The descent offered a quiet miracle; the Kaveri River glimmering beneath the mist, palm groves stretching in feathered rows, and red earth streaked with morning rain. From the air, Tamil Nadu looked less like a map and more like a living mandala; waterways curling like ink around ancient villages, temple towers rising like prayers cast in stone.

The car ride south to Thanjavur was a journey through living contrast. Women in jewel-toned saris balanced brass pots with effortless grace, school children skipped along road edges, their laughter rising through the hum of scooters and the chants from passing roadside shrines. Jasmine garlands dangled from auto-rickshaw mirrors, mingling their scent with diesel and turmeric. Roadside vendors stirred steaming pots of sambar, while temples old as time flickered by like mirages behind banyan trees.

India didn't whisper. It surged; wild, fragrant, thunderous. And yet, to Selena, it still felt like home.

She had booked a room at Svatma, a heritage hotel nestled within a restored 100-year-old Tamil Brahmin house. From the moment she arrived, she felt like she had stepped into a sanctuary layered with memory.

The architecture was an homage to Tamil classicism: red oxide floors, pillared courtyards, teakwood swings, and carved lattice panels filtering sunlight like sacred geometry. The air smelled of sandalwood, lotus petals, and freshly ground coffee. Every corner whispered intention, from the brass oil lamps to the veena music floating in the reception hall.

A staff member in a cotton dhoti greeted her with a jasmine-scented towel and a copper cup of panakam; a sweet-spiced tamarind and jaggery drink once offered in temples. The welcome was not performative; it was ancestral.

Her room was a blend of simplicity and reverence: high-beamed ceilings, a hand-carved four-poster bed, antique writing desk, and a balcony overlooking a quiet garden where mynah birds hopped between banana trees. On the desk lay a small welcome card with an inscription in Sangam Tamil:

"To return is not to arrive, it is to remember."

Selena stood for a long time by the open balcony doors, watching temple bells ring in the distance, the call of a nadaswaram drifting through the air like a half-forgotten tune.

The sun filtered through the gauze curtains, warm against her skin. She could still taste the ginger in the panakam and the scent of the jasmine in her hair. Somewhere in the streets below, temple drums began their midday rhythm, echoing the beat that had guided her across oceans.

Before leaving Lamu, Professor Elijah Mutua had connected her with a colleague in India's National Epigraphy Centre who confirmed that a new research corridor had opened under Brihadeeswarar Temple; ancient mural work not yet digitised or shown to the public. More importantly, a set of obscure Chola-era inscriptions made reference to an emissary who returned from "Zanzibar" with sacred fire rites adapted to Tamil cosmology.

Zahara. Ariyama.

The names weren't craved in stone. But Selena could feel their imprint; subtle, resonant, undeniable.

She opened her bag and removed the copper seal from its wrap of silk. It pulsed faintly, as if sensing proximity to its origin. Tomorrow she would walk to the Brihadeeswarar Temple, not to ask questions, but to listen.

This wasn't just the land of her ancestors.

It was the river's bend; where vow and voice became one.

River Bend – Thanjavur, Brihadeeswarar Temple Grounds, Nightfall

The sun had long dipped below the horizon when Selena arrived at the banks of the Kaveri. Dusk had laid its soft shawl across Thanjavur, and the air was thick with the hum of insects, distant conch calls, and the low percussion of temple drums preparing for the night aarti.

She stood at the edge of the river bend, where tradition said the divine feminine gathered with the force of a thousand moons. The Kaveri, ancient and slow-moving, shimmered in bands of starlight. Along its banks, women in cotton sarees lit small clay lamps and set them afloat on the water, whispering prayers that stretched backward and forward through time.

To her right, the Brihadeeswarar Temple rose like a mountain carved from the breath of gods.

Even in darkness, the temple glowed.

Built over a thousand years ago by Raja Raja Chola I, it was a marvel not just of architecture but of imagination. The vimana, the towering central spire, soared nearly 66 meters into the night sky, crowned by a single stone weighing over 80 tons. Lit by subtle uplighting and flickering oil torches placed along its base, the temple shimmered in warm bronze hues, each carved panel catching shadow and flame like script drawn from fire.

Granite lions and dancers adorned its walls. Inscriptions lined the base like coded memory; names of queens, architects, poets, warriors. And among them, a curious entry that referenced "a fire brought from the western edge of the great sea... brought by the one who left and returned unnamed."

Selena's breath caught.

This temple wasn't just a monument to devotion. It was a map; carved not across continents, but in vibration. She could feel it in the stones beneath her feet.

The River Kaveri, too, was more than just water. In ancient Tamil cosmology, it was the lifeblood of the Chola heartland, a sacred feminine artery that nourished not just fields but philosophies. Poets once called her the "Mother of Waters" and believed her bends marked places where the divine met earth most directly. Even today, farmers chanted to her during planting, and pilgrims bathed in her currents before seeking darshan at the temple.

As Selena sat on a granite ledge overlooking both temple and river, she felt held by something immense. Not just by the landscape, but by lineage. The Kaveri was not just a river. It was a recording device. An eternal listener. A carrier of vows.

And tonight, it was listening to hers.

She removed her sandals, letting her feet touch the stone. The earth was still warm from the day's sun, pulsing faintly beneath her soles.

Wind moved through the temple corridors behind her like a sigh. Somewhere in the darkness, a nadaswaram began its plaintive tune; reedy, reverent, winding through the air like a serpent seeking its source.

Selena closed her eyes and listened.

Not with her ears, but with her skin. Her breath. Her memory.

The vow had come full circle.

Temple Corridor, Brihadeeswarar Temple, Inner Sanctum Archives – Next Morning

The morning air was honey-thick with incense, dust, and the promise of something ancient stirring beneath the surface. Brihadeeswarar Temple awakened slowly, not with noise, but with ritual: the sweep of brooms across stone, the rhythmic clang of metal pots being washed, the murmur of priests in ochre robes preparing the sanctum.

Selena arrived just after sunrise, escorted by a local historian from the Tamil Nadu State Epigraphy Department. Through Professor Elijah Mutua's contact, she'd been granted rare access to the lesser-known mural corridors; portions of the temple closed to tourists, shielded not out of secrecy, but reverence.

She stepped barefoot across the cool flagstones of the inner prakaram, the stone corridors that ringed the temple like a spinal cord. The scent of sandalwood and sesame oil clung to the walls, mingling with the metallic tang of old inscriptions.

To her left, an ancient wall inscription in Grantha script caught the morning light. It spoke not of war or conquest, but of a returning emissary. A woman. Not named, but described as "she who bore the western fire, in whom the vow was sealed, and through whom the lotus awoke again."

Selena reached out and touched the stone. It hummed beneath her fingers.

The corridor narrowed. A priest with kavi cloth around his waist silently opened a wooden gate carved with flame motifs, nodding for her to proceed.

Inside, the light dimmed. This was the Chitra Mandapa, the painted gallery.

Even in the half-light, the murals pulsed with colour. Mineral pigments; lapis, turmeric, ash, copper dust, clung to the stone like breath held for centuries. There were gods, sages, dancers, and queens. But in one small alcove, barely visible unless you knew where to look, a different figure emerged.

A woman, cloaked in deep indigo, holding a scroll in one hand and a serpent-lotus staff in the other. Around her feet, the stylized waves of a sea. Above her head, the silhouette of a ship with twin lion-head prows.

Selena inhaled sharply. The scroll. The sigil. The crossing.

Her knees bent involuntarily. She knelt before the mural as if drawn down by gravity not of the body, but of memory.

Behind her, the priest said quietly in Tamil,

"She is not a goddess. She was one of us. The woman who returned."

Selena closed her eyes. The air inside the corridor was thick with devotion; not loud, not performative, but vibrational. The sound of a conch echoed in the distance.

And in that moment, something clicked.

Not Vellichi. Not Mayilai. Not Zahara. But, Ariyama.

The final incarnation.

The return not to end, but to begin again.

Her breath slowed. The seal in her pocket pulsed with heat. And the murals around her shimmered.

The trance was not coming. It was already here.

....

Dream Trace – Ariyama's Return, Chola Heartland, Circa 11th Century CE

The heat shimmered low over the banks of the River Kaveri. It was not yet midday, but the sky pulsed silver and gold, thick with monsoon scent and the scent of wet sandalwood. From the mud-brick steps descending into the river, the sound of bronze vessels being dipped and lifted echoed like a ritual heartbeat.

Ariyama stood ankle-deep in the water, her palms cupped, raising a shallow bowl of river to her forehead.

The vow had returned with her.

Her robes were woven of deep blue, embroidered with a thread so fine it caught the light like rain. Around her waist, a sash carried the serpent-lotus sigil. Her hands bore ink marks not of caste, but of carriage; script drawn on skin as prayer, as portal. Her hair, braided in copper thread, was bound with a single plume of white egret feather, symbol of a return without conquest.

A small group waited on the riverbank; scribes, temple stewards, one female priestess dressed in ochre. Behind them, the tower of the Rajaraja Chola's newly consecrated temple rose like a mountain of carved flame.

The Brihadeeswarar Temple. The place her journey would end, and begin again.

One of the stewards stepped forward, bowing slightly. He did not ask her name.

He simply said, "The corridor is ready."

Ariyama nodded, stepping out of the water. Her bare feet pressed into the red earth, leaving wet footprints like calligraphy across time.

She walked through narrow corridors, torchlit and lined with freshly etched murals. She paused only once, laying her palm on an unfinished panel.

"I will be remembered not as a goddess," she whispered in Old Tamil, "but as the one who carried the scroll and came back."

Then she reached the mural chamber.

In her arms, wrapped in cloth scented with clove and ash, was the final scroll. It carried no instructions. Only pattern. Only presence.

She pressed it into a niche carved behind the mural, a hidden chamber sealed with wax and rice paste. Then she stepped back, bowed three times to the mural-in-progress, and turned toward the exit.

Outside, the conch blew. The river moved. And far above the temple tower, three hawks circled, a sign.

The vow was now whole. Not buried. Not hidden. Remembered.

The Return of Ariyama – Present Day

The temple corridor was colder than Selena expected.

Even with the morning heat rising outside, the inner sanctum stayed still; stone walls whispering with condensation, inscriptions breathing through time-worn chisel strokes. She stood beneath a frieze of celestial dancers, their limbs mid-movement, each anklet and earring captured in the stone with reverent detail. But it wasn't their beauty that held her, it was the gesture.

One arm raised in abhaya — protection.

The other lowered in varada — offering.

Not a deity. A dancer. A guardian of thresholds.

The mural ahead had been recently revealed, a fragment that had eluded restoration teams for years. Now cleaned and partially visible, it showed a procession; a woman cloaked in indigo, scroll in hand, standing between sea and shrine. In one corner, the triadic sigil, serpent, lotus, trident, was faint but unmistakable.

The priest who had escorted her into the restricted corridor stood silently beside her.

"She was called Ariyama," he said softly, "in the old inscriptions. It is said she returned with fire, but spoke little. She taught gestures, rites... left no descendants. Only memory."

Selena swallowed hard. The air felt thick, not just with dust but with knowing.

She knelt before the mural and placed the copper seal at the base of the painting. It didn't glow. It didn't shimmer. It simply settled, as if it had found its way back to where it began.

In that silence, she heard the river.

The same pulse she'd heard in Lamu. In Yazd. In Rome. In Alexandria.

And deep inside her, she felt the spiral complete.

Not as a loop, but as an unfolding.

Outside, the Kaveri flowed gently. Her waters were low in this season, yet still moving patient, purposeful.

Selena stood barefoot at the river's edge once more, now with no questions.

Not seeking signs. Not looking for maps.

She understood it now. She was the map. Each lifetime had left an imprint:

- Mayilai, whispering the first vow into ink and flame.

- Vellichi, dancing fire into scrolls.

- Zahara, sealing sacred codes into coastal rock.

- Ariyama, returning home to offer silence instead of prophecy, and now,

- Selena, remembering them all in the only way memory survives through presence.

She bent down, pressed her palm to the earth, and whispered the name she now remembered as her own.

The river shimmered. The air stilled. And in that pause between past and breath, she heard it:

The river had always known her name.
It was only waiting for her to speak it back.

Selena's Diary Entry

Field Notes – Thanjavur, South India

Mission:

Return to Thanjavur, the heart of the Chola empire, to trace not a scroll — but a soul thread. Discovered the mural corridor beneath Brihadeeswarar Temple. Confirmed inscription referencing a Tamil emissary returning from Zangzibar (East Africa) with sacred rites. Recognised self — Ariyama — as final incarnation before this life. Vow not buried, but fulfilled.

Chakra Thread:

Sacral: Creation and continuity — the flame carried through lifetimes now re-enters the body.

Heart: Reverence and release — compassion for all that was remembered and all that was lost.

Crown: Illumination — integration into unity consciousness; no separation between vow and vessel.

Selena's Reflection:

I didn't arrive here to find proof.

I came to remember the sound of the river inside me.

Each life had left a symbol — flame, scroll, chant, seal — but they were never fragments. They were syllables of the same sacred language.

The vow was not buried in temples or oceans. It lived through each incarnation, waiting for the voice that would finally remember.

I see now that Ariyama was not an ending.

She was the bridge — the moment the fire laid itself down to rest in the river.

And I am the continuation of her stillness.

The spiral has unfolded.
The vow is fulfilled.
The silence speaks.

Repeated Phrases:

"The river remembers."

"The vow returns where it began."

"She who left, returns unnamed."

Keywords:

- Ariyama.
- Serpent–Lotus–Trident.
- Fire Rites.
- Temple Mural.
- Brihadeeswarar Temple.
- Seal Returned.
- Sacred Continuum.
- Chola Lineage.
- River Kaveri.
- Spiral Complete.
- Vow Fulfilled.
- Homecoming.
- Stillness as Completion.

Chapter Eighteen – The Keeper of Names

Gangaikonda Cholapuram *(Ancient Chola Empire Central)*, **Tamil Nadu – Present Day**

The road narrowed as Selena left Thanjavur behind. Her driver turned onto a rural stretch where rice paddies shimmered like emerald silk, their irrigation channels catching the last of the sun in molten ribbons. Water buffalo moved slowly, their wet hides reflecting the sky's bruised violet, while herons rose startled into the air at the hum of the passing car.

The landscape blurred past, and Selena leaned closer to the window, feeling the familiar vibration stir in her chest, the same pulse she'd felt leaving Lamu, now stronger, as if the land itself were calling her home.

When the car slowed before the northern gates, the air thickened with incense and drumbeats. She stepped out, slipped off her sandals, and walked barefoot toward the sandstone corridor. The heat beneath her feet was not just warmth, it was recognition. She wore a simple cream kurta and an indigo shawl that caught the wind like a whisper of dusk. Her hair was loosely tied at her nape, not from vanity, but instinct, as though some part of her already knew the corridors ahead demanded stillness, not spectacle.

Before her rose the vimana of Gangaikonda Cholapuram, the temple Rajendra Chola I had built in the 11th century to mark his conquest of the north and the ritual bringing of Ganges water south. Its sandstone walls glowed like embers in the dusk, the carvings alive in the shifting firelight. Where Brihadeeswarar in Thanjavur towered with imperial grandeur, this temple whispered differently. Its carvings were subtler, its corridors narrower, its voice one of veiled endurance rather than dominance.

The sandstone glowed like living fire in the dusk. Garlands of marigold and jasmine hung from the doorway, their scent mingling with lamp-smoke and wet earth. A breeze stirred through the colonnades, carrying faint notes of nadaswaram and drum from a courtyard wedding far behind her.

To the east lay the Chola Ganga, the great reservoir filled centuries ago with water carried ceremonially from the northern Ganges. Its surface shimmered like hammered copper under the rising moon. Selena felt her pulse quicken.

As she entered the cool corridors, something stirred. Not vision. Not dream. Memory, awake.

Her fingertips brushed the walls, and the sensation surged; Ariyama's feet walking here centuries earlier, garlands in hand, lips whispering invocations. Selena felt the overlap of selves, the echo of anklets on the same stone her feet now pressed.

It rattled her. The burden of knowing one's past, she realised, was not the drama of visions but the quiet shock of recognition in stone. Every step deepened the ache; was this remembrance a blessing, or a weight she was not meant to carry?

She pressed her palm against the stone. Her breath trembled. The temple felt less like architecture and more like a body remembering her.

Temple Whisper – The Amulet Call – Present Day

At the reservoir to the east, the Chola Ganga, she saw a woman waiting.

She wore indigo cotton, her braid silvering into her shawl, her posture neither humble nor commanding but assured. Around her neck hung a copper amulet, serpent coiled mid-motion, lotus blooming at its crown.

This was Meenakshi Devi, a local historian and oral-keeper whom Professor Elijah Mutua in Lamu had introduced her to via a chain of scholars. The message had been cryptic: "She guards what paper cannot."

Meenakshi spoke softly, her Tamil accent rippling through her English:

"Most come here to look. Only a few come to listen."

She lifted the amulet. "This has been carried by women of my family for nine centuries. Through famine, invasion, and exile. They were never told its origin, only to keep it. To wear it close."

Selena leaned closer, recognising its twin to the seal in her own bag.

"The copper," Meenakshi continued, "is no accident. When Rajendra returned with the waters of the Ganges, copper plates were inscribed to record his conquests. But some plates, unrecorded in archives, carried no land grants, no tributes. They carried only symbols like this one."

Selena felt her pulse quicken. "And the keepers?"

"Women. Always women. Temple singers, midwives, archivists in silence. They kept the amulet not as relic, but as continuity. Through lifetimes, through generations. When the scrolls burned, the seals endured."

Selena's own seal pulsed faintly through the silk pouch. The air between them quivered, two vibrations meeting.

And suddenly the hum deepened. Her chest grew tight, her vision swimming. The temple itself seemed to lean in.

The woman's voice lingered even after she had gone, her words about the amulet folding into the silence of the temple like incense smoke. Selena stood alone in the corridor, fingertips brushing the carved lotus patterns on the granite wall.

The amulet in her palm pulsed faintly, as though alive. Not with heat, but with vibration—a hum that seemed to match the rhythm of her own heartbeat. She pressed it to her chest, and for an instant, it was impossible to tell whether the sound came from stone, skin, or memory.

Her knees buckled slightly, and she steadied herself against the wall. The air thickened, curling with sandalwood and camphor, the same scents she had breathed earlier—but stronger now, almost suffocating. The temple was no longer still. It was vibrating.

She closed her eyes.

And when she opened them again, the light had changed. The corridors were the same, yet not. Torches flickered where electric bulbs had been. The air was heavy with chanting. Somewhere beyond, drums thundered like a second heartbeat.

She was no longer walking as Selena.

She was kneeling as Ariyama.

The vow had pulled her through.

....

Dream Trace – Ariyama's Final Rite, Gangaikonda Cholapuram, Circa 11th Century CE

The temple breathed like a living organism. Its granite walls radiated warmth, soaked in centuries of oil lamps and ritual chants. Carvings of lions, lotuses, and dancing deities shimmered in the firelight, their shadows rippling like spirits in attendance. Selena stood there, but not as herself.

Her breath came deeper, slower, as the dream thickened. Her body throbbed with recognition.

The air was heady with incense; camphor, sandalwood, and ghee-fed flames. Drums thundered, veena strings vibrated, and the low drone of conches echoed across the sanctum. And then, the crowd parted.

The great Chola King Rajendra entered.

He wore a crown of gold studded with rubies, sapphires, and diamonds that seemed to hold constellations. His torso was bare, glistening with sacred ash smeared across his chest in broad white stripes, a tiger-claw pendant resting at his heart. Around his waist, a silk dhoti shimmered crimson and gold, pleated like waves. His gait was slow, regal, the weight of empire woven into every step.

Behind him walked his retinue: generals, scribes, and temple guardians. Yet it was the king who held the room. His presence was not merely political; it was cosmic.

Ariyama knelt near the altar, her role not one of ruler but of keeper. The amulet pulsed at her side, hidden beneath ceremonial robes. She could feel the vibration in her bones, the hum that Hindus called mantra. Not words to be spoken. Vibrations to be embodied.

As the king approached the sanctum, a chant began. Not in Tamil alone, but in layered tongues; Sanskrit, Prakrit, even syllables from lands across the sea. Ariyama moved with the rhythm, her hands folding into mudras, her body resonating with each vibration.

The sounds were not chanted aloud; they thundered through her body like lightning through a copper rod. Each syllable wove itself into the temple walls, into the flame, into the very stone beneath her knees.

Selena, inside Ariyama's body, felt her modern consciousness reeling. The burden of such knowing pressed heavily upon her ribs. She wondered: Was it mercy or punishment to remember all this? In her present life, she had chased history. But here, she was history. The vow was not a story. It was her marrow.

The king raised his right hand in blessing, his gaze falling on Ariyama. Not as ruler to subject, but as guardian to guardian. A flicker of recognition passed between them, silent, timeless, unrecorded.

The sanctum's flame roared higher, blue at its heart, gold at its rim. Ariyama placed her palms to the earth, bowing low, not in submission but in resonance. She was not merely keeping the vow. She was becoming it.

Selena's body in the present trembled on the temple floor. Her spine arched with the current of mantra, her skin damp with sweat, her breath uneven. Yet she was not afraid. The vibrations of the temple had caught her, held her, remembered her.

The dream blurred at the edges, but the feeling lingered. She was not alone. The vow was alive.

....

Copper Seal Activation – Present Day

The copper seal warmed in Selena's palms, its surface no longer inert metal but alive, humming with the rhythm of her own breath. She held it at her heart, her spine erect, eyes half-closed as the temple air seemed to thicken around her.

It began as vibration. Low. Steady. Not external sound, but an inner hum, the resonance she had felt earlier in trance now echoing in her waking body. She had read countless texts on chakra theory and sound resonance, yet none had captured this. Books described mantras as syllables of power, tools for focus, but here, the sound was not hers to control. It was the body's ancient language, reactivated. She finally understood; each vibration was not a call to an external deity but an awakening within the self, a precise frequency that opened a gate between matter and consciousness. The seal wasn't amplifying her energy, it was tuning her to the original harmony she had once known.

She placed it at the water's edge. The surface rippled outward in perfect concentric circles.

Her breath steadied. She whispered:

"Lam. Vam. Ram. Yam. Ham. Sham. Om."

Each word was a key. Each unlocked a chamber in her own body.

- *Lam* anchored her spine, heavy, red, earth-bound.

- *Vam* spiralled into her pelvis, silver, fluid, creative.

- *Ram* sparked in her navel, golden fire, a sun of agency.

- *Yam* spread like green light across her chest, tenderness unarmoured.

- *Ham* surged through her throat, a blue river, voice unblocked.

- *Sham* tightened into her brow, indigo sight, an eye opening within.

- *Om* crowned her skull with violet flame, dissolving her edges into the cosmos.

Energy didn't climb only upward. It moved both ways; a current rising, another descending, meeting, circling, feeding. She felt tethered to earth and yet drinking from the stars.

For the first time in her waking life, she did not feel fractured across histories.

She felt whole.

The universe was not outside her.

It was moving through her.

Final Integration – The Shadow Path

When the vibration quieted, Selena rose, still barefoot. She walked the shadow path cast by the temple's vimana, moonlight striping the stones.

At the far end, beneath a carved arch, he waited.

Her soul twin.

She froze. Until now, she had only seen him in meditation. But here, awake, in the temple's sanctified field, the veil thinned.

Soul twins, she now realised, were not fantasy of romance but resonance of vow; one soul in two vessels, split to carry weight across lifetimes. They appeared when recognition was needed, when the vow risked fracture.

He did not speak. He only lifted his palm. She raised hers. When they met; not flesh to flesh, but vibration to vibration, the hum surged again, clear and anchoring.

His gaze held no demand, only presence. Two halves of one vow, aligned.

For the first time, Selena did not chase the trail.

She was fully aware that she was the trail.

She no longer traced the vow.
She carried it.
And the land finally bowed in return.

Selena's Diary Entry

Field Notes – Gangaikonda Cholapuram, South India

Mission:

To understand vibration not as metaphor but as mechanism. The Copper Seal activated more than memory—it awakened the body's original circuitry. I finally grasp what no text could teach: mantra is not repetition, but resonance. Each syllable aligns a current; each chakra is a portal that responds to sound as the body's first truth. Through the seal, I didn't summon energy—I remembered how to listen to it. The sacred was never lost; it was simply untranslated until the body spoke it again.

Chakra Thread:

Root to Crown: full alignment through vibration and breath. Energy rising and descending in a single continuum; not ascent but circulation. Balance through remembering, not striving.

Selena's Reflection:

The hum no longer frightens me. It moves through me like recognition—an ancient voice returning home. I used to think enlightenment meant light; perhaps it's simply remembering the vibration you already carry. The sound is not separate from silence. They complete each other.

Repeated Phrase:

"The body remembers what the soul once sang."

Keywords:

- Copper Seal.
- Mantra as memory.
- Sound-body awakening.

- Frequency.
- Chakra ignition.
- Inner language.
- Vow reactivated.
- Wholeness.
- Integration.
- Silence after sound.

Chapter Nineteen – The Flame She Carried

Kanchipuram: The City of Thousand Temples, Tamil Nadu, India – Present Day

The Journey Inward

Once the radiant capital of the Pallavas, later refined under the Cholas, it was where philosophy, architecture, and silk converged like the threads of the cosmos itself. Scholars called it Kanchi-pura, the City of Light; a city that housed not only shrines but entire schools of metaphysics, where poets debated dharma and artisans etched the Upanishads into stone.

For the Cholas, this was no ordinary seat of power; it was their spiritual axis. From here, they commissioned temple blueprints that mirrored planetary geometry. Here, queens like Kundavai Chola founded monasteries that trained both male and female scholars, the forgotten custodians of flame and ink.

Even today, every street in Kanchipuram seems to end in a temple, every threshold hums with prayer.

Selena had studied it once through maps and manuscripts. But this time, she wasn't arriving as a researcher. She was walking into the Chola pulse itself, the junction where history became living frequency.

The train traced its path through the heartlands of Tamil Nadu, gliding past paddy fields glowing green under a sapphire sky. Occasional bursts of temple towers, gopurams glazed in timeworn colours rose like myth from the landscape, each one whispering old names and older stories. The rhythmic chug of the engine had grown into a meditative pulse, a mantra of arrival.

Selena sat by the window, chin resting on her knuckles, her notebook closed on her lap. She wore a sapphire cotton kurta with silver paisley embroidery, chosen deliberately for both practical and reverent, paired with soft-soled sandals. A light scarf in shades of turmeric and charcoal was wrapped loosely around her shoulders. Her usual black field bag lay at her feet, worn now from months of movement.

She was not the woman who first stepped onto the sands of Alexandria. That version of herself had been searching; wide-eyed, unsettled, driven by clues and compulsions she barely understood. Now, as the train curved toward Kanchipuram, she felt the shift. She was no longer chasing fragments.

She was arriving whole.

The Hotel of Names – Saratha Vilas Residency, Kanchipuram

Her driver met her at the platform holding a modest placard: "Dr. Selena Ravencroft – Epigraphy Team." A half-hour later, she stood before the Saratha Vilas Residency, a meticulously restored 19th-century Chettiar mansion turned heritage hotel. Originally built as a guesthouse for royal Chola envoys and later used during the French missionary period, the villa was a living text of syncretic history. Columns of polished granite rose beneath teak eaves carved with guardian motifs. The scent of old sandalwood lingered in the halls.

Her room overlooked a courtyard garden, where frangipani trees bloomed despite the September heat. Inside, the décor blended colonial-era furniture with bronze lamps and traditional Tanjore paintings; one of which, she noticed, depicted Sundara Chola receiving a scroll from a veiled emissary, a detail that caught her breath.

She settled into a carved rosewood chair and poured herself a cup of cardamom-infused tea from the brass kettle left on the counter. A deep exhale escaped her lips as she opened her notebook, flipping past pages from Alexandria, Lamu, and Rome.

Her itinerary was precise:

– 3:30 PM: Visit Ekambareswarar Temple

– 4:00 PM: Epigraphic study of copper plates under pre-cleared access

– Evening: Personal meditation, flame vigil

She traced her thumb over a drawing she'd sketched weeks ago; the serpent, lotus, and trident, etched again and again into the margins, as if her hand knew something her conscious mind had not.

She closed the notebook softly. Her breath deepened.

A vow was not something she carried anymore. It was something she lived.

The Temple of Convergence – Ekambareswarar Temple, Kanchipuram

Selena arrived by auto-rickshaw just after the heat of the day had broken, the sun now slanting gold across the temple's grand eastern gopuram; a 57-meter high tower, carved with thousands of divine forms. The temple complex was immense, its origins predating the Cholas but later expanded under their patronage, especially by Kulottunga I, who had reinforced it as a cosmological anchor point.

Here, it was said, the five elements converged:

- **Earth**, embodied in the lingam formed from sacred sand by Parvati herself;

- **Water**, from the ancient temple tank fed by subterranean channels;

- **Fire**, in the eternal flame kept alive by priestly lineages for centuries;

- **Air**, whispering through the inner sanctums where no fans or devices stirred the atmosphere;

- **Space**, held in the open mandapas, where the heavens passed unbroken over head.

The famed 3,500-year-old mango tree stood near the inner sanctum, its four branches said to bear fruit of four distinct flavors, one for each Veda. Standing at the threshold, Selena realised why Kanchipuram had been called the navel of the South. Every vibration here, the clang of bells, the scent of camphor, even the footfall of devotees, seemed tuned to a single harmonic. The temple wasn't built around the flame; it was the flame, crystallised into geometry.

The scholar in her, noted the engineering precision: granite lintels aligned with solar solstices, an axis connecting sanctums like vertebrae along a cosmic spine. The seeker in her, though, felt something else entirely, the deep pulse of Earth rising into human breath.

For a fleeting moment, she wondered if the Cholas had ever intended these temples to be visited the way museums were; silent, distant, observed. Or if they were meant to be entered as bodies are, with surrender and heartbeat.

When she finally stepped into the shadowed corridor, she wasn't merely entering architecture; she was stepping into frequency.

Under special access arranged by Dr. Suresh, the same mentor who had first handed her the Lamu fragment months ago, she was guided by a local epigraphy scholar into a sealed-off sub-shrine newly unearthed beneath the stone mandapa. Layers of time seemed to fold inward here; soot from ancient lamps, broken terracotta votives, and beneath them all, ten copper plates, delicate as leaves but etched with force.

The inscriptions spoke of a returning emissary from Zanzibar who brought with him not wealth, but a ritual of flame, a vow carried by fire.

It was a throwaway line in the inscription, a curious anecdote.

Until she saw the sigil. Serpent. Lotus. Trident. Her breath stopped.

The same triad she had chased across three continents. Only now, it wasn't a relic. It was a mirror.

She documented the plates, of course. Took high-res scans and rubbings for the grant. But her heart beat with something deeper, not discovery but Recognition.

Dream Trace – The Soul Assembly – Timeline of Selena's Past Life Vow, Circa 950 CE

That evening, she returned to Saratha Vilas Residency just before dusk. The lamps were being lit along the corridor, casting long shadows across the red oxide floors. She placed the scans carefully in her bag, set her phone to airplane mode, and pulled the blackout drapes across the old wooden shutters.

Tonight was not for data.

She lit a single ghee lamp, which you bought from the temple, beside the Tanjore painting of the veiled emissary, seated herself on the mat, and closed her eyes.

Her breath deepened. She chanted softly an ancient Tamil verse gifted to her by Mayilai in a dream weeks ago. As the chant dissolved into silence, her body cooled while her mind slipped through thresholds. Time thinned. She felt the border between breath and memory dissolve. The sound of the fan overhead became the echo of a conch. The creak of the old teak floor became the heartbeat of drums. The veil between centuries didn't tear, it softened, like silk meeting skin.

Her pulse aligned with a rhythm she recognised but had never learned.

Somewhere, beyond the mind's horizon, the ancestors were gathering.

She opened her eyes to another century.

950 CE. Inside the Soul Assembly.

She stood barefoot on a stone floor veined with fire. Above her, no sky, only shifting constellations of memory and vow.

This time, the ancestors did not arrive one by one. They came together, a full circle of selves. Vellichi in her storm-dyed

239

sari. Zahara cloaked in desert silence. Ariyama holding a staff of ink. Mayilai smiling with ash across her brow.

No scrolls. No flames in the hands. Instead, they stepped back.

And she stepped forward.

A mirror rose before her, not made of glass but of possibility. In it, she saw not her face, but all her faces. All her timelines. All the women she had ever been and all she had ever protected.

The voice of her soul twin rose, no longer a whisper but a bell:

"You were never the archive.

You are the fire.

The vow was not to protect it.

The vow was to become it."

As she reached toward the mirror, it did not shatter, it absorbed her.

And in that moment, the lines between scholar and seeker, between fragments and fullness, dissolved.

She was no longer translating the vow. She was the transmission.

....

The Return – Kanchipuram, Before Dawn

The temple drums woke her before the sun. Birds stirred on the frangipani tree outside her window. The ghee lamp had burned out. But the flame within her remained steady. Bright.

She opened her notebook. She would report on the plates; a previously unknown ritual link between Tamil Nadu and East Africa, hints of cultural memory embedded in bronze and trade.

But there was another truth, a quieter one:

She was no longer chasing history.

She had become its living voice.

She left Kanchipuram before breakfast, the streets still misted with early incense and distant chant. Her scarf fluttered as she stepped into the car.

She did not look back. She did not need to.

The road back to Chennai shimmered with early heat. Farmers were already in their fields, ankle-deep in water, chanting softly to the Kaveri for a generous monsoon. Selena watched them from the car window, her reflection layered over theirs, past and present folding together.

She thought of the conferences ahead, the papers to write, the quiet disbelief of colleagues when she'd present the copper plates and the ritual parallels. Yet this time, she wouldn't argue. She would simply offer. The proof was no longer in data, it was in presence.

For the first time, she saw that her professional life had never been separate from the sacred. Research was a form of prayer; scholarship, a discipline of devotion.

As the car merged into the highway, the first rays of sun struck the rear-view mirror, catching her eyes. The light flared; a perfect, fleeting reflection of the same flame she had carried from temple to temple, continent to continent, lifetime to lifetime.

It wasn't following her anymore.

It was hers.

And as the landscape unfurled, she whispered inwardly —
May the vow travel further than I can walk. May the flame
never need another keeper.

Selena's Diary Entry

Field Notes – Kanchipuram, South India

Mission:

To reach the source — not the origin of the vow, but the understanding of it.

Kanchipuram was never merely a destination; it was a convergence, the place where spirit, intellect, and lineage fold into one current. Here, at the heart of the ancient Chola consciousness, I understood that the work was never to preserve the flame, but to become its expression.

The copper plates, the inscriptions, the temples — all were languages of the same vow. But the truest record was always the body, remembering through vibration what words could never archive.

My task is no longer excavation. It is integration — to live scholarship as devotion, and devotion as research.

To stand in the field not as observer, but as vessel.

Chakra Thread:

Heart + Solar Plexus: Compassion fused with purpose. The flame's intelligence anchored in will, illuminated by love. The final balance between knowing and being.

Selena's Reflection:

Kanchipuram taught me that enlightenment is not ascension — it is arrival.

All this time I believed I was tracing lost histories; I was really tracing my own remembering.

The vow was not waiting in the past; it was breathing beneath every moment I resisted stillness.

I no longer need to chase evidence. I am the evidence — the living continuation of what could not be erased.

The soul twin was never a destination or an ending, but a mirror. Every encounter, every field note, every chant — all of it was the universe reminding me that fire is the memory of light learning to return to itself.

Repeated Phrase:

"I was never meant to guard the flame. I was meant to become it."

Keywords:

- Copper plates.
- Kanchipuram / Ekambareswarar.
- Eternal flame.
- Serpent-lotus-trident.
- Soul Assembly.
- Dream trance.
- Guardianship.
- Embodied archive.
- Five elements.
- Arrival.
- Transmission.
- Now.

Epilogue – Where the Flame Settled

Location: Unknown Coastal Town
Time: Later

She walks through a small coastal town, the kind left off maps and travel guides, where the sea meets the land without ceremony. The streets are half-asleep this time of day, sun filtering through palms in molten shafts, falling across chipped stucco walls and faded murals of forgotten saints.

She's here on a research sabbatical, officially. A short ethnographic survey of pre-colonial maritime routes and shared ritual practices along India's southeastern corridor. It's real work, peer-reviewed and university-funded, her name printed neatly on the project brief.

But that's not why she came.

Not really.

She rents a modest room above a spice merchant's home. The shutters open to the sea, and when the tide recedes, she can hear the clink of shells shifting like prayer beads in a hidden hand. When it rains, the whole house smells of turmeric, cinnamon, and salt. The ceiling fan wobbles, uncertain, but she's grown fond of its imperfection. It's the kind of place that hums rather than speaks; gentle, self-contained, patient.

Each morning begins the same way. She walks barefoot to the beach before sunrise, tea in hand, tracing the curve where water meets sand. No rush. No performance. The horizon blushes lilac, then gold. The world breathes. So does she.

Later, she meets local elders for interviews, fishermen, midwives, retired teachers, recording oral histories about tides, trade winds, and the chants once sung to launch boats toward Africa. The stories never stay linear. They drift. Someone always remembers a grandmother who could predict monsoons by the colour of moonlight, or a song that changed direction mid-verse depending on which way the wind blew. Selena doesn't interrupt. She lets memory lead.

Afternoons are slower. She writes brief notes, then stops. Walks instead. Some paths end in mangrove thickets, others at half-sunken shrines where marigolds float in brackish pools. The air buzzes with insects and incense, and sometimes, she swears she can hear faint drumming beneath the hum of waves. Her bag is lighter now; the old journal, gloves, scanners all packed away. What she carries can't be catalogued.

Children sometimes run past her, drawing tridents in the air like it's a game. Sometimes she catches the word flame in a song she doesn't understand. She never chases it. It always knows where to find her.

Evenings arrive softly, like an exhale. She sits on the verandah of her guesthouse, sipping tea heavy with ginger and cardamom. The lamp beside her flickers, small but unwavering. The horizon folds into copper and rose. Waves hush against the shore; crickets begin their patient chorus.

She's not waiting for visions now. She's learning the rhythm of ordinariness, the grace in repetition. There is holiness in small acts: rinsing the cup, closing the window, writing a single true sentence. Each gesture feels like prayer disguised as habit.

Sometimes, she thinks of the women who came before, Mayilai, Vellichi, Zahara, Ariyama, not as myth or memory, but as frequencies woven into her breath. Their strength moves through her without ache now. The fire that once consumed her curiosity has gentled into warmth.

Then, a soft chime from her laptop.

She smiles, unsurprised.

Inbox (1):

Subject: *Follow-up on Copper Plate Translations – Re: Kanchipuram Data*

From: Dr. Gabrielle Cheng

*University of Melbourne – Department of Archaeology and Cross-Cultural Epigraphy

Dear Selena,

Just finished reviewing the Kanchipuram files you uploaded.

We're fascinated by the inscriptional reference to the Zanzibar emissary, especially that ritual phrase you highlighted. It opens up a whole new line of inquiry regarding transoceanic cultural exchange in the 10th century.

Let's discuss at your earliest. Also, we're greenlighting a wider study if you're willing. Your work is helping us reimagine what "archives" even mean.

Warmly,

G. Cheng

Selena reads it twice. Then closes the laptop, not out of avoidance, but reverence.

The scholar in her still exists, but she no longer leads. The seeker does. Her research isn't about recovery now; it's about rhythm. The data, the dates, the discoveries, they matter, but only because they hum with something living beneath them.

She leans back in her chair, watching the horizon melt into sea. The air carries salt, jasmine, and the faint scent of clove smoke from a distant fire. The light around her has a strange mercy, golden but grounded, as if even the sun has begun to exhale.

Tomorrow she'll write back to Gabrielle, yes. She'll agree to the new project. But she'll do it slowly, as she's learned to do everything now; with stillness, with tea, with gratitude.

She understands it at last:

Some knowledge must be studied.

Some must be lived.

And some, the most sacred kind, must be remembered through silence.

Below, a fisherman hums an old sea song, its syllables stitched from Tamil and Swahili. The melody rises, falters, then steadies again, like breath. Selena closes her eyes and lets it find her.

Some archives are not kept.
They are carried. Lived. Embodied.
And sometimes, they even send emails.

About the Author

Soraya Radfield is an author of emotive suspense dramas. Her work blends fiction with a deep fascination for history, mystery, and the layered truths we carry.

Soraya grew up in Kuala Lumpur, Malaysia, and has since travelled, lived, and worked across many countries before finding her home in Australia. A later-in-life interest in ancient history, archaeology, and untold stories sparked an unexpected creative path. Though she studied Quantity Surveying and Construction Management, her natural curiosity and passion for understanding how the past shapes us, led her toward fiction.

Having journeyed multiple times through Turkey and other historically rich regions, Soraya found herself captivated by the emotional residue left in cities, ruins, and forgotten maps. A turning point came when she realised the research and reflections she'd been quietly collecting over the years had formed the bones of a novel. That novel became The Last Conversation.

Writing, she discovered, is as deeply satisfying as the research that fuels it. Through storytelling, Soraya explores memory, identity, and the fragile intersections of history and hope.

She believes in following your curiosity and turning your passion into your most rewarding hobby.